DR CLOCK'S
LAST CASE

and other stories

DR CLOCK'S
LAST CASE

and other stories

RUTH FAINLIGHT

Published by VIRAGO PRESS Limited, April 1994
42–43 Gloucester Crescent, Camden Town, London NW1 7PD

*A CIP catalogue record for this title
is available from the British Library*

Typeset by Florencetype Ltd, Kewstoke, Avon
Printed and bound in Great Britain by
Mackays of Chatham PLC, Chatham, Kent

CONTENTS

ACKNOWLEDGEMENTS

BANANAS, ed. Emma Tennant,
Quartet, 1977
Dr Clock's Last Case

CAUGHT IN A STORY: Contemporary Fairytales & Fables,
ed. Caroline Heaton & Christine Park,
Vintage, 1992
The Fish-Scale Shirt

CRITICAL QUARTERLY vol. 30, no. 3, 1988
Three Ambiguous Visitors

NEW STORIES no. 4, ed. Elaine Feinstein & Fay Weldon,
Hutchinson in association with the Arts Council, 1979
Mid-Term

THE PARCHMENT MOON, ed. Susan Hill,
Michael Joseph, 1990
PENGUIN BOOK OF MODERN WOMEN'S SHORT STORIES, ed. Susan Hill,
Penguin, 1991
Another Survivor

PENGUIN MODERN STORIES no. 9, ed. Judith Burnley,
Penguin, 1971
Soir de Fête & The Expatriates

PENTHOUSE vol. 8 no. 4, 1973
Dr Clock's Last Case

PICADOR BOOK OF THE BEACH ed. Robert Drewe,
Picador Australia, 1993
The Fish-Scale Shirt

TWELVE: Stories by Famous Women Writers, ed. Denys Val Baker,
W. H. Allen, 1978
Another Survivor

Earlier versions of *Pleasure* and *Houses* (under the title:
Yvonne and Rachel) were published in Ruth Fainlight's collection of
stories, DAYLIFE AND NIGHTLIFE, Andre Deutsch, London, 1971.

I

A WIZARD'S ROBE PATTERNED WITH STARS AND MOONS

The playground was surrounded by tall, stained brick buildings, and the young of the neighbourhood's nations and races ran and shouted on its concrete. Ellen imagined Martians hovering above, wondering what those darting small creatures in the deep pit below might be. She was the only one to notice them, and her upturned face would be their first sight of a human being. Being almost ten and a half, she felt too grown-up to play with the little ones, but the older children made her painfully aware of her small size and immature appearance.

That summer, Ellen thought about Martians a lot. She would like to see some. One night she dreamed of a pale, white-bearded giant in a tall hat and a wizard's robe patterned with stars and moons, who floated over the city and loosed a rain of pinky-white stuff like sticky popcorn or small dead shrimps that clung to her clothes and skin. She could remember a hollow reverberating voice, perhaps the wizard's, louder than any siren, warning to take cover – but not whether she had ignored it out of bravado and curiosity, or had just left it too late. Though she hammered on door after door along the wide empty streets, pleading for shelter, no one would let her in. She screamed as the burning corrosive flakes settled as soft as snow and bit into her bare arms and legs, then woke in a cold sweat, quite different from the usual hot discomfort of New York summer nights. The dream seemed to be connected to those half-comprehended reports of battles and bombing raids she heard on the radio, and the fact that she and her mother and younger brother were here while her father was on the other side of the world.

Recess ended and they went inside. One wall of the classroom was window, banks of glass so dirty it was hard to tell the difference between the frosted lower panes and the higher ones that only gave a view of bricks. A complicated network of manila rope to open and shut them hung like the rigging of a pirate ship. Ellen imagined scrambling to the crow's nest and scanning the horizon for rescue. She wasn't making up for work missed last year because she hadn't been here then, and in any case, always got good grades. The library had been locked for the summer, so she couldn't borrow a book. It was a relief when one of the young women helpers handed out sheets of cardboard and glass and said they were going to make pretty pictures to take home to their mothers.

The oblongs of glass were crudely stamped with the silhouette of a boat (nothing as grand as her pirate-schooner), with thick black wavy lines for the sea, and a shoreline and clouds. Sheets of shiny metallic paper were passed around, then the teacher showed them how to put it between the painted glass and cardboard backing. Ellen persuaded two of the others at her table to exchange some of their paper for bits of hers, and ended up with a blue sea, silver clouds, and crumpled golden sand. She could imagine her father joking about how awful it looked, but the realisation that her mother would praise the picture with exactly the same uncritical intonation and expression she would use if shown a masterpiece, for a moment made it seem almost as magical and beautiful as the teacher said.

They must have been invited to the party because of some gallant, secret and dangerous exploit of her father's, she decided, studying the embossed square of thick white card that arrived with the morning's mail. Her mother laughed when Ellen explained this theory to Hugo, and told them not to be so silly. New York was full of children whose fathers were on war service, and they couldn't all be heroes. But Ellen and Hugo exchanged looks of faith and resignation, like true believers faced with an apostate.

There was still the fresh damp smell of water sluiced through the gutters by the early morning street cleaners, and the sun had not yet mounted high enough to reach the sidewalk as they hurried between the tall apartment blocks.

'What can I wear to the party?' Ellen asked anxiously, running ahead to look into her mother's face without either of them having to slow down.

'One of your dresses will do very well.'

'Can I make myself one? You won't need to buy anything for it. I've got it all worked out.'

'What on earth are you talking about?' Her mother's voice was distracted and irritable. They had reached the entrance to the school. 'Now don't forget to find Hugo and give him his sandwiches. And the two of you go straight to Aunt Lena's this afternoon. No hanging around on the street, understand?' A neighbour had agreed, for a price, to supervise the children during those difficult hours between the end of school and her return from the mid-town office where she worked. With so many women in a similar position – rusty from years of being housewives, and not able to manage on what the authorities regarded as an adequate allowance – she had been lucky to find a job.

A jumble of images from the movies was all that Ellen had to draw on, when she tried to imagine the elegant hall where the party was being held. A movie star was guest of honour, the invitation revealed, so she knew there would be lots of photographers. If only she could get her picture in the papers . . . Then it wouldn't be merely a matter of Hollywood directors fighting each other for a chance to work with her. The whole family would be able to move from their one-and-a-half-room apartment into a mansion, and her mother have nothing else to do except advise and admire her triumphant daughter. And that was just the start. The President would certainly want to have a private fireside chat with such an extraordinary girl, and doubtless arrange for Ellen's father to fly back from wherever he was to deliver a front-line report. Whether she would actually be able to stop the war . . . Here, the unreeling film must have snapped. There were no images at all for a moment.

Everything depended on the marvellous garment she was going to make from the large ecru-coloured lace curtain which Lena had given to her after noticing how much Ellen admired its deep fringed border of birds and flowers, when they had been straightening her closet one afternoon. 'You take the old thing if you like it so much,' she said, putting it into a brown paper bag. 'It's the only one left out of six I got when I was married. I haven't used it for years.'

Her mother's attempts to dissuade her from wearing a curtain to the party were unsuccessful. Ellen pondered every detail, lying awake in the stuffy room where the three of them lived and slept. It would be a shame to cut the piece of fabric – better to let it to hang from her shoulders like one of the Greek or Roman togas in her history book. She'd always made clothes for her dolls, and a few weeks before a dirndl skirt for herself had turned out all right. Imagining the grand transformation, she eased as far away as possible from the body of her mother, who moaned now and then in her sleep and became hotter and hotter as the night progressed.

It didn't matter that none of the neatly suited men and smiling women in the reception line paid any attention to her. There was so much to notice that it was better not to be distracted. Ellen stared at the shining parquet floor, elaborate chandeliers and gilt pilasters with tall mirrors between, the waiters and waitresses in sober uniforms and the tables covered with plates and glasses ranged along one side of the vast room. The ceiling was so high that voices sounded lost and faint across the empty central space into which no one had yet ventured.

The noise level rose as speakers of different languages among the families of Allied servicemen competed for audibility. Then, by some mysterious process of communication, they all became aware that the guest of honour had arrived. Children quietened and moved closer to their mothers, and those who had been circulating with trays of food and drink stopped and stared in the same direction towards a small dark-haired woman with a pretty, heavily painted and bad-complexioned face, who slowly turned her head in a wide arc and made each person feel that she had looked directly at him or her alone. Ellen understood at once that this was the essential quality of stardom. A touch on the elbow brought her back to the present. A man standing in front of her said, 'Come over here, into the picture.' It was all beginning to happen, she thought.

Like representative beneficiaries of a charity, a group of guests was being formed to commemorate the occasion. 'Stand here,' he directed. Ellen heard a woman mutter, 'Don't you think she looks a bit odd?' but no one objected when she pulled from her mother's grasp and squeezed into the front row. There was a fusillade of flashbulbs, then it was all finished. The actress and her entourage moved briskly away, and the rest of the group drifted off like parts of an organism that no longer have any function. One of the men nearby called, 'Milly, for heaven's sake!' in a delighted tone of voice, and clasped her mother's hands. 'I didn't know you were in New York.'

Ellen hadn't seen her mother smile like that for ages. 'Yes, these are my two babies.' She gestured them closer. 'You wouldn't recognise her after so much time,' she laughed, and added, 'She loves to dress up.'

'Charming.' His glance passed rapidly over Ellen and then back to her mother's face. 'Come over and meet the others.'

Ellen turned to where Hugo had stood a moment before, but she was surrounded by strangers, all of whom seemed to have a great deal to say, though not to her. She might as well have been on another planet.

'Have you had anything to eat yet, dear?' an elderly English woman in a fussy brown hat enquired. 'I expect you must be feeling a bit lost.' Ellen followed towards the refreshment tables, and munched her way through several slices of cake, darting hostile stares at anyone who looked as if they might begin a conversation.

She was released by Hugo's voice in her ear. 'We're going home,' he said, grinning happily. 'Terrific ice-cream. Come on, Mum's by the door.'

'Who was that?' Ellen demanded.

Her mother responded with a shrewd and critical look. 'An old friend of your father's. He's over here doing some war work.'

'I'm glad my Dad's a soldier, anyway,' Hugo commented as they waited for the elevator.

Next day at school Ellen insisted that she didn't want to take the glass and silver-paper picture home but refused to say why. Later when the teacher told the class how Uncle Sam was helping all the people in Europe and described the falling houses and storms of flame menacing London children at that very moment, then played the record of a fulsome contralto singing 'Land of Hope and Glory', Ellen couldn't hold back any longer. As they all watched the tears run down her face and heard her sob, 'Daddy, Daddy', that little demon, chin on fist and faunish legs crossed, who always perched somewhere up in the top corner of the scene observing her performance, chuckled with admiration. Even though she moaned louder and squeezed her eyes tight shut to wipe out sight and sound of him, she knew he was there in his robe of moons and stars, her most reliable ally and familiar.

8

THE SCRATCH

In winter there was a carpet on the floor, but at the start of summer, Uncle Roscoe would roll it back and heave it on to his shoulder, ends slowly sinking behind and before, and grinning like a Lascar stevedore, carry it to the cellar.

The linoleum underneath had a wide border and tightly flowered centre printed in an old-fashioned formal design – Brussels carpet I think they called it – in a range of shades from cream through beige and brick and tan to darkest brown. I knew every flourish, repeat and irregularity because once a week my task was to get down on my knees and wash the kitchen and living-room floors. That was how I found it, a gouged-out crooked crescent inches long.

The bearer of evil tidings, I might as well have been the guilty party. My house-proud aunt's distress was unnerving. To soothe her, and prove my innocence as well as my skill, I promised miracles.

Uncle Roscoe went down to his basement workbench to mix cement and glue, then tamped the ugly rip until it rose smooth and level. A box of oil paints had been my chosen birthday present. I squeezed dabs of umber and sienna, zinc white and cadmium yellow, from the smooth metal tubes on to the red-stained wooden palette and tentatively dragged streaks of pigment towards each other with a stiff new brush. I crouched, then knelt, then spread-eagled flat, licking sweat off my upper lip and wrinkling my nose to stop my glasses sliding.

9

All that August, during the hottest hours of afternoon, sunlight sifted through the screens like little heaps of still-warm white ash from last year's summer-camp fires. My brother and I would pull the curtains across every window in the living room and sit cross-legged and barefoot on the cool linoleum, playing gin rummy. If you looked hard you could just see, like the stain left by a dropped twig or the shadow of a scar, the dull mark of the mended scratch on its patterned surface.

GOLDENROD

In the empty lot opposite, the goldenrod. I walked down the porch steps and crossed the narrow road. Blossoming spikes reached as high as my shoulders, and as I pushed through them the loosened pollen made me sneeze.

Blue sky and gold flowers and pale dusty earth. Green leaves beginning to dry at the edges and curl inwards, rust-blotched by the end of summer. A space that seemed vast enough to hide from everything, among the densest clumps of bushes at the centre, to read and dream or watch how ants veered around the shiny pebbles, how beetles crawled up jointed grass stems and the mantis moved its legs. I had learned not to go barefoot because of the red chiggers that burrowed under the skin between your toes and had to be dug out. When I took my sandals off at night, the top of each foot was stained by the sun into an elaborate pattern of white and brown.

Now it was September, and I watched the goldenrod harden and darken. School had started a week ago and I was still in love with the same arrogant, spectacled boy I had not seen since June. After class, we took up all our old arguments about God, Marx, and the meaning of life, just where we had left them, as if there had been no break. I had arrived home so charged with refutations and unpresented evidence that I immediately sat down to write him a letter. I sealed the envelope and cut across the lot to the next street and the nearest

11

mailbox. As soon as it had fallen through the slot I knew I had made a fool of myself.

The afternoon seemed even hotter than August, but maybe that was because I was wearing my new sloppy-joe sweater and a pleated skirt instead of T-shirt and shorts. There must be some way to get the letter back.

If any neighbours passed they would be sure to ask why I was standing there. I retreated into the vegetation keeping the box in my line of sight. The mailman was due about now. As I moved restlessly through them, drifts of disturbed pollen rose from the tall plants. But even after I explained why it was so important, he refused to let me search for my letter among the others. Nothing I said would sway him. He grinned and walked away muttering, 'Crazy kid!'

The dull yellow expanse of the field hummed and vibrated. In spite of the new school clothes I threw myself down on the hot ground between the bushes, and later blamed my swollen eyes and tear-streaked face on the powdery torment of the goldenrod.

JOSEPH'S VISIT

The two houses stood stranded between the last street where whites lived and the beginning of the black district – a no man's zone of empty lots and decrepit farmsteads whose fields had been sold off decades before. The small Virginian town was already jammed with army people and war-workers when my uncle was sent there to supervise a new factory. Suddenly, for the duration of the war, he had become head of a family consisting not only of himself and his wife but also his wife's sister and her two children. Finding anywhere at all to live was a stroke of luck, so he had bought one of the badly built pair. The other was occupied by Walter and Dolly, their baby boy and daughter Diana, and Rover, the red setter dog. Not yet thirty years old, the couple already looked slack and middle-aged.

My aunt soon developed a maternal attitude toward the younger woman. 'She doesn't know how to look after a family, poor girl. I guess her mother never taught her.' Wearing the starched housedress of flowered cotton, sleeves and neck modestly decorated with coloured rickrack, which she changed into after coming home from the office, my aunt was the picture of domestic efficiency. She would praise Diana until I burned with jealousy. 'A little angel! To think she's cursed with a father like that.' Walter was a policeman. He kept guns in the house and did target practice in the basement, bet on horses, and spent the weekend drinking beer and shouting, effusively and more and more irritably, at wife, children

13

and dog. As the Saturday evening sky darkened, Dolly's expression became nervous and placatory. She would pull the children towards her, then hurry them to bed out of Walter's way.

I was eleven when we moved there, then I was twelve. On the far side of the empty field opposite, behind some half-dead trees that must have been planted in the last century, stood a row of pleasant suburban houses. Tall clumps of weeds grew at the field's centre, where my brother and I played with the children who lived there, but they would never ask us to go home with them. Was it because we were merely transients war had washed up and would soon float away, or did they know that my aunt talked across the fence to our black neighbours and even invited the boy from the house nearest ours to come for milk and cookies? When this happened we always stayed inside – a decision arrived at with no need for discussion. Even Diana could not be included.

Though two years younger than my brother, and half my age, Diana pleaded to join in everything we did. There was no one else for her to play with. When her father was home, she came to us to avoid him. I knew it hurt her even more than Dolly must have been hurt, when Walter shouted and slapped her mother's face. Silently, Dolly would lift a hand to the livid mark down one cheek as if to soothe and hide it, and stare with wide eyes at her balding, tense-featured husband. 'Why don't you say something, you stupid fat cow?' I heard him scream one Saturday afternoon. But later, when Diana had gone back home, the sound of their laughter rose into the darkening golden sky like the flight of birds into the trees' black silhouettes.

It was a particularly hot summer, and the coolest place to be was the cellar. Dirty and barefoot, wearing the minimum allowed, we sat on the wooden steps leading down from the kitchen, or on the half-broken wicker chairs near the gal-vanised iron wash-tubs, planning the rules of our secret club and the fearsome initiation rites Diana must undergo if she wanted to become a member. Her dark blonde hair curled

14

damply around her worried, excited little face as she listened. We were too soft-hearted, or perhaps too timid, to subject her to those comic-book-inspired ordeals, but enjoyed tormenting her with vivid descriptions of what lay in store.

When Walter was out of the house, we went to Diana's for a change of scene. I watched everything Dolly did. She seemed the archetypal married woman – not like my aunt who was so much older and had no children, nor my mother, whose husband was away on the other side of the world. Dolly's husband was omnipresent. She was young, she had children, she exuded the smell of marriage which perhaps was this very compound of beer and babies which permeated the untidy house.

My aunt often took a rest after lunch. If I wanted to talk to her then, it meant entering a realm in which a man would have been entirely out of place. Everything was delicate and ordered, the way I imagined the room of a great lady, or a nun. Dolly's bedroom was the opposite, I discovered, when I followed her into it one day. This was the lair of a couple. A dirty pair of socks lay beneath a chair, a large black police boot was visible among the dust-balls under the bed, and the half-open closet seemed crammed with masculine garments. The few cosmetics and trinkets on the dressing table were pushed to one side as if to indicate Dolly's awareness of having no special rights in the room.

'I'm so tired,' she said, crawling heavily on to the unmade bed, pulling off her dress and slumping back against the creased pillows. 'I'd really be thankful if you'd mind the baby for a little while.' She raised an arm behind her head, exposing a luxuriant tuft of damp dark hair. Her slip stopped short of dimpled knees and fell between resigned-looking thighs, and I tried not to stare where its thin fabric was darkened at hip level. 'Have some milk from the icebox and take something to eat for all of you,' she muttered, and rolled on to one side as if to evade my gaze.

Every second or third Saturday night I babysat next door. It

15

was supposed to be an opportunity to do my homework but, as soon as Walter's car pulled out of the drive, I would turn on the radio to listen to The Hit Parade. If for some reason their departure overlapped the start of the programme, it was hard to conceal my impatience. I had covered a special notebook with flowered waxed paper, and used it only to write the lyrics of each new song – though sometimes I had to wait for another hearing to get them word-perfect. Banal and insinuating, I felt sure they expressed the secret meaning and deepest wisdom of life – which it seemed more appropriate to learn in this house rather than my own.

When the programme ended and I had forced Diana up to bed, I would usually read my library book. One evening I forgot it and, without much hope, searched for a substitute. On a top shelf in the kitchen, pushed far back into the corner, were half-a-dozen tattered paperbacks. When Walter and Dolly walked through the door I was so absorbed that I had not heard the car pull up in front of the house.

Dolly took the book from my hand without a word, but Walter at once began to fulminate. 'Don't make a fuss,' she pleaded. 'She's only a kid, she didn't understand anything. You don't want them to know what sort of books you have, do you?' He was not to be deflected. Muttering righteously, and keeping a firm hold on my arm, he marched me across the short distance between the houses. But thin strips of light outlined the doors of my aunt's and uncle's bedrooms, and the room I shared with my mother was in darkness. 'You've had a lucky escape,' he said, then laughed and added, 'You're a forward little kid,' and gave me a pat on the rear before he released his grip and disappeared.

There was an epidemic of rabies in town, and one oppressive morning, Rover began to run in circles around the back yard making strange laboured noises rather than barking, white foam falling in large flakes from open jaws on to the

16

burnt, straw-pale grass and the sweat-darkened red of his coat. Dolly called us into the house and latched the screen door shut. My brother knelt on a chair to look over the window-sill, then turned to me, eyes piteous, a greyish pattern of mesh on his nose and forehead where they had pressed against the screen, and asked, 'They won't kill him, will they?'

It was not long before a patrol car arrived and Walter and a colleague, bizarre paunchy figures in their sombre uniforms, emerged and walked carefully across the yard through the shimmering midday heat. The moment they entered the house, the baby began to cry, and my brother tugged at Walter's arm, demanding, 'What are you going to do to Rover?'

Walter looked hot and uneasy and about to lose his temper. 'That dog is sick, understand? He's a very dangerous animal. If he bit any of you kids you'd die. It would take a long time and it would hurt a lot.'

'Can't you make him better?' my brother insisted. 'I'll take care of him. I'll feed him every day and give him water. I won't forget, you won't have to keep after me.'

'Leave me alone.' Walter shrugged his arm away and went into the bedroom. A few moments later he reappeared, breaking and loading a shotgun. In spite of Dolly's efforts, the baby was still screaming. Diana and my brother moved closer together, and closer to Dolly. 'Now stop it, all of you,' Walter commanded. 'That dog has got to be killed. It's a danger to everyone, and only a sissy would make a fuss.'

The screen door slammed behind him. No one moved until we heard the first shot, and then another immediately after. Rover had not made a sound. The baby fell silent as Diana and my brother began to cry, and her sobs and his muffled choking almost obscured the sound of Walter and his fellow officer driving away.

Another man was sitting on the porch with Walter and Dolly the next Saturday evening, and I wandered around our side of the shared yard, trying to see who it was through the dusk, and hear what they were saying. 'Come over and meet my brother,' Dolly called. I did not hurry, wanting to give the impression that I was well used to meeting strange men.

'This is Joseph.' Dolly beamed with complacent love. He was dressed in a black suit and open-necked white shirt, and looked a few years the younger, with curly black hair and an almost handsome face. He stood up and bowed his head ceremoniously, then sat down again, flexing his knees and spreading them wide apart before carefully raising each trouser leg. His gestures were deliberate, even exaggerated. Beams of light through the windows glinted on his sweaty face as he stared up at the soft, star-scattered sky.

'Do you live near here?' I enquired, when no one broke the silence.

'No, no, little lady.' He laughed as if I had said something amusing. His reaction was puzzling, and set me on my mettle. I would not accept being treated like a child. I heard my aunt and uncle coming out on to our porch to enjoy the evening coolness, their words clear on the still air.

'Are you visiting?' I persisted.

'I can't recall when I last met such a fair young lady.' He spread one hand across his white shirtfront like a stain, and leaned forward, ignoring my question. His hands were wide, with stubby fingers and black-rimmed nails. Nevertheless, I was delighted to have his attention. 'My sister told me of the lovely wee maid next door,' he went on, 'but I did not look to have my expectations surpassed so greatly.'

'Stop it, Joseph,' Dolly laughed. 'Joseph has a way with him,' she confided proudly. 'He always had the gift of the gab.'

'Pour out another beer for me, Dolly,' Walter interrupted, glancing at his brother-in-law with much less appreciation.

'And for your baby brother as well, sister dear, oh fairest of matrons,' Joseph added.

'I think you've had enough,' Walter said. 'I know what happens next when you start talking like that.'

I turned from one to the other, a fixed smile of polite interest on my face. What did Walter mean? I had never heard one grown man talk to another in that tone. But perhaps it was normal behaviour between people like Walter and Joseph, and Joseph's statements were compliments to be acknowledged with all possible grace.

'My dear young lady – I may call you that, I hope? – I want to thank you for your kindnesses to my sister, and your companionship. Oh yes, she has told me!'

I was losing touch with the sophisticated character I wanted to be, and could not think of an appropriate answer. Joseph stood up, tottered slightly, then righted himself as he walked down the steps towards me.

'You mustn't be standing there while I'm sitting down. Please take my chair.' He placed a hand on my bare arm, then leaned his head on to my shoulder and began to hum an indistinguishable tune.

'Joseph!' Dolly quickly followed him. 'You bad boy! He's a bit tired,' she explained, amused but uneasy. 'He travelled a long way today.' She took firm hold of her brother's arm, trying to lead him up the steps again.

'Come over here, dear, it's getting late,' my aunt called. 'Goodnight, Dolly,' she added in a decisive tone of voice.

'Oh – ' I began to protest.

'Yes, it is late,' Dolly agreed, interrupting me. 'We'll see you in the morning.'

Joseph reached out for one of my hands and raised it to his lips. A strong smell of beer and sweat came from him. 'Goodnight, my vision of delight,' he said loudly, a baffling note of laughter in his voice. Without a word I lifted my chin and walked self-consciously across the dividing line between the two properties and up our porch steps.

'Come inside, dear.' My aunt followed me into the kitchen where Mother sat writing her nightly letter to Daddy. 'That man was drunk, darling,' she said putting her arms around me. 'He didn't mean to tease you.'

19

'He wasn't teasing me. He was very nice!'

That would make everything terrible. Nothing worse could ever happen. My uncle was grinning, my mother and aunt looking at me with such strange, understanding expressions. It was unbearable. If I didn't get away immediately they would see the tears that already had begun to overflow my eyes.

THE DOVE DRESS

Looking down at the printed pattern on the dull mauve fabric stretched across my legs, how much this dress reminds me of one I wore when twelve or thirteen years old. That also had an anachronistic style which made me feel in disguise: a dove-coloured nun rather than the adventurer I believed was my true nature, as if already I sensed an affinity between the two roles.

I bought this dress at a fashionable shop. The other was my aunt's. By the time I claimed it, it might well have been twenty years old. The loose cotton, soft from being washed so often, was gathered into a deep yoke and the cuffs of wide puffed sleeves. Like this cloth, it was printed with small white blossoms. But there were touches of other colours, particularly the golden-apricot stroke along a petal of each flower, which I especially liked.

Weekdays I dressed like everyone else: pleated woollen skirt, sloppy-joe sweater (sometimes buttoned down the back) with matching knee-high socks, and saddle-shoes because, according to my aunt, moccasins didn't give enough support. But Saturday morning, wearing that dress more often than not, I took the bus from the corner of our street to a class for school-children at the city Art Gallery.

Those hours in the studio with its high skylight, the air dusty with charcoal and pastel, scented by fixative, thick with the silence of concentration, were the best time of the week. After-wards, reluctant to leave, I went downstairs to the main galleries. If the shadowy room of plaster copies of famous statues was empty, I would sit down and try to draw them.

That day I had positioned myself against the plinth of a conveniently placed gladiator and started to rough-in the forms of Rodin's *The Kiss* on a clean leaf of my sketch pad.

'That's pretty good,' said a soft Southern murmur over my shoulder. I turned to meet the gaze of a slight youth in military uniform whose velvety stubble of dark hair made me feel a disturbing combination of repulsion and the desire to rub the palm of my hand across the top of his head.

My friends could recognise the signs that indicated rank, but I had never managed to absorb the information. Neither was I good at judging age, though he did not seem much older than the senior boys at school. Flattered by his comment, I was troubled by the problem of how to reply. As often before (and since) I thought how much more satisfactory it is to imagine something happening than to be presented with the actuality. 'You really can draw,' he continued. 'I wish I could draw like that. Does it come naturally or do you have lessons?'

Now he had asked a question I could tell him about the classes. Talking made me feel less awkward. 'Are you interested in art?' I did not have high expectations of soldiers. They were necessary to fight the war, I knew well enough – otherwise I equated them with the sort of young men who got drunk and whistled at girls, made jokes about niggers and Yids, and guffawed when the word 'art' was mentioned.

'I guess I am interested,' he admitted. His uncertainty increased my confidence. I twirled a lock of hair forward and pushed my glasses up my nose. 'I'm going to be an artist. I'll probably go to Paris to study after the war.'

'You're really cute, you know that?'

I saw no connection between being cute and being an artist, and the flush that mounted my face confused and angered me. 'This is a famous statue,' I stated decisively. The two figures yearning towards each other glowed whitely. He looked down at my drawing.

'Would you let your boyfriend kiss you like that?'

It was easy to avoid his trap. 'Oh, I just started to draw this one because our teacher was talking about it today.'

He changed the subject. 'You look like a real artist. That's the sort of dress I always imagined an artist would wear.'

'I'll have to go now. My aunt is waiting for me.'

'I was going to invite you for an ice-cream soda.' He sounded disappointed. I remember thinking how jealous my friends would be when I told them.

The dark and silent gallery with its varnished panelling, the pale greasy gleam of plaster casts like dough gone hard, and two young people talking intently, seen small and distant – he with his short cap of furry hair and olive drab uniform and she in the dove-coloured dress which she stripped off and threw into the back of the closet as soon as she got home – is what this dress evokes.

MALTED MILK

The thick sweetness of malted milk was the flavour of those mornings when I would sit with my best friend at the soda fountain in the corner drugstore and share a milkshake before another day at T. J. Junior High. I remember her sallow serious face with the cowed expression of a daughter of Jehovah's Witnesses, and going with her family once to the wooden chapel where their congregation worshipped – though I have entirely forgotten her name.

Almost forty years later I was trying to find that drugstore, that school, the vacant lot we cut across on our way home every afternoon, and the house or even just the street where my mother and brother and I had lived with Aunt Ann and Uncle Roscoe.

The row of modest houses, jerry-built for an influx of war-workers, which ours began or ended (depending on your point of view), the derelict farmhouse opposite with its yard full of broken machinery, the scrubby tract of ground behind half-dead trees where my friends and I imagined rapists lurked, and the unexplored region beyond – it all returns in meticulous detail. But the name of the street and the number of the house escaped me, and studying the local map was little help. I recognised the main thoroughfares – Glebe Road, Columbia Pike, Wilson Boulevard – but none of the intersecting gridwork between struck more or less familiar. The schools we went to during the war (I mean the Second World War, not those others their names evoke: Thomas Jefferson Junior High, Patrick Henry Elementary, Washington-Lee High) were still marked, and I thought they might be a start.

Outside the Metro station, nothing gave a clue about which direction to take. It was a cold bright morning. I craved the comfort of sugar, the support of malted milk, but could not see a café or drugstore, only a row of telephone booths near a DIY warehouse. The best idea seemed to call for a taxi. Ten minutes later a low caramel-coloured car pulled up. The driver had the broken-veined complexion and wistful expression of a drinker. Neither he nor his car were in their prime.

I knew it would be hard to explain what I wanted, but hadn't expected him to state with such assurance that T. J. wasn't there any more, nor the High School either. 'I used to go to those schools,' I protested, adding, 'I haven't been back since then,' as though if I could gain his interest and sympathy he might conjure them back into existence.

'You went to Washington-Lee?' He turned to get a better look at me. 'The old building was beat up by the time I got there. Worn out by kids. That must have been – when was it? – about '53.' I realised that his eyes were a beautiful blue, and that he was the younger. 'Just before I went into the Marines.' 'And I've been away for years.' How lucky that he had come in answer to my call, rather than another driver.

'I think T. J.'s a sort of community centre now.' We cruised past a row of stores that must have been there then. A shabby movie house looked familiar, and the drugstore on the corner we were turning. 'I think I recognise that.' I felt ridiculously excited. 'Sure, we all hung out round there, but they took away the soda fountain years ago.'

'Do you remember Smoky Hollow?' I wondered if it was a good idea to ask. The ones my aunt wanted me to be friends with avoided the place, but I was sure he had known it well – a sandy depression in a weed-grown field behind the playground where certain people would go when they cut class to drink from hip flasks, smoke pot, and make and change relationships

26

of love and power. The driver nodded. Through the rear mirror I saw the corner of his mouth curve, as though he didn't smile often. 'It's just a truck-park now. Nothing left of Smoky Hollow.'

A half-constructed underpass blocked the direct route. Not much of the old High School had survived extension and alteration. He walked around the site with me then shook his head disbelievingly. 'I live in this town, but I just hadn't realised.'

We circled and quartered the area where the small house had been. Only a few of the appropriate age and style still stood. Most of the buildings were new red brick low-income apartment blocks. Even the street plan had altered from what the driver remembered. I chose a house almost at random.

There was no problem in placing my aunt's pots of blackish-purple and pale yellow pansies along each side of the paved path or up the concrete steps to the front door; and the little porch at the back, with the garbage cans underneath, could easily have been the eyrie where I'd brooded about my future. On the other side of that white-painted dormer window might be the same room Mother and I had shared. But looking at the photographs I took then, I am not convinced. It is more disconcerting to think I passed the house and did not recognise it than to accept that it had been demolished.

The driver hunched in his seat smoking while I prowled with my camera. 'Where to?' he asked as I got back into the car. I felt jaded and irritable. 'I'd like a malted milk. Will you have one with me?'

'Sorry, lady. I've got another job waiting. But I'm obliged to you. Otherwise I probably wouldn't ever have known that it isn't like it was.'

AN OLD LADY

The man next door was out with his mower again. Though the window was closed and the air-conditioner switched on, she could hear the idiot buzz of its engine, and if she sidled over to the window, pulled back the curtain, and took a squint through the screen and glass, she could see him as well. There were no fences between the yards, but everyone knew the exact boundaries of their own property, the last inch over which they had legal rights. All very well to go outside and smile and bob a response when he called, 'Hello there, Mrs Miller. Wonderful day!'; to do the same with the neighbours on the other side. She knew damn well, just as well as they did, in fact, that the borders of her yard ran from the clothes-line up to the row of grapefruit trees, then down along the far side of the flower bed. Yes, that flower bed was hers, Morton had dug it especially, and many a time she'd tried to get something to grow in it apart from these big tropical bushes they all loved so much – something like pansies, or forget-me-nots: some sweet little flower to remind her of before she'd come to this place – but that pest of a neighbour's dog would never leave them alone, or else they died from the heat.

Years ago, when Morton was still alive, when they'd fixed up this bungalow with as much enjoyment as if they were newly-weds in their very first house, she'd managed to grow flowers and the people who lived next door didn't have a dog. But everything was different now. She wished she was deaf, not to

29

have to hear the yapping of that stupid dog, or the lawnmower, especially when he was doing her a favour and cutting her grass as well as his own. She might as well be deaf, on top of all her other complaints. She wasn't good for anything these days: just enough life left to crawl around the place, do a bit of dusting, and flop down panting afterwards. Her eyes weren't up to much either, and as reading had been her most effective technique for passing the time, it was a sore deprivation. They'd taken the car away after Morton died, when the time came to renew the insurance, saying she wasn't fit to drive any more. She had to rely on that same next-door neighbour, and be grateful to him for everything: errands, shopping, trips to the doctor.

It was amazing how often she couldn't avoid having to go next door, squinting up at them like some ancient horror (she knew what she looked like, no good trying to fool her and tell her she wasn't enough of a sight to make you sick to your stomach, an old witch covered with moss and fungus) and wheedle a lift into town. That's what her whole life had come to: begging and dragging on from one day to the next. She was stuck out here in this so-called paradise and – apart from the neighbours, a pleasant couple who seemed to have adopted her as the focus for their surplus affection and concern – the only people closer than a thousand miles were her fat slob of a cousin and his lazy, good-for-nothing wife. Luckily they had retired to another town, and it was years since their last quarrel and her determination never to speak to them again.

When Morton died they'd heard about it somehow, but they weren't going to get into her good books again just by sending a big bunch of flowers. Oh no. She knew better than that. She knew that if you gave that type an inch they'd take a continent. She wished she'd sent the damned flowers back. The first grief of widowhood had included dreadful shaking bouts of rage. Perhaps that was how she'd managed to get through those days. Now the rage had fallen in like a collapsed volcano and she was smothered under the ash, a bitter taste of ash in her mouth as if she had thrust her head into the little metal urn and was chewing it all up, mumbling over the last physical remains of her husband. Every day, whatever else might be neglected, she carefully dusted and polished that urn.

She had a sister, and cousins, nieces and nephews with children, but she couldn't be bothered to keep in touch. They wrote now and then or phoned a few times a year; some of them even hurt by her refusal to respond. They meant nothing to her now. Her only reaction was a sort of sour envy at their capacity to be hurt, and a faint dying memory of what such emotions had felt like. The last one left to her was irritation.

When she and Morton moved here she'd still loved children. It seemed as though the less suited a pair were the more likely they'd spawn a brood: which was why there were so many criminals, and drunkards and madmen – all products of feckless ignorant neglect, as she often remarked. She would have devoted herself to a child, a little angel whom she could protect from the cruelty and deceit of the world. Their childlessness had been a great sadness to them both. With so much free time after retiring, she'd done what nice old ladies do in all the stories: baked up big batches of cookies and called the neighbourhood youngsters into the house to eat them, and have a drink of milk or maybe lemonade as well. She knew she was quite a local character, but hadn't realised how unnaturally pressing her interest appeared. The children would escape as soon as possible – pockets laden with cookies, giggling nervously as they promised to come back next day for more.

Something similar happened with the parents. They liked the Millers, especially Morton. He'd been good for a drink and a game of cards any time, but she had tried to dazzle the men with her superior culture, to teach the wives all the little niceties they lacked. Nevertheless, they'd accepted her. It was obvious that she didn't know how much she antagonised people, and anyway no one could doubt her good intentions.

All her life had been like that, and now there was nothing

left except to think about the past, she was slowly and painfully comprehending the fact. Morton's job had taken them to every part of the country, and the responses of the new arrival had become habitual. She'd always felt she was living in the wrong place, among the wrong people, that somewhere else she would be appreciated and her true nature allowed to flourish. There'd been no time or energy for making new friends once she was married. Some demon had compelled her to try to be the best at everything: the best stenographer, the best cook and homemaker, the best-dressed woman in her crowd, the one who'd read the latest book banned in Boston and was the wittiest and brightest and the most fun. Even though she was sure that half the time he didn't know what she'd been talking about, when they got back home after a party, Morton's praise seemed to be the prize she had strained for; the only reward there ever was.

It was ten years since they'd moved here, and she was as lonely as at the start. She didn't even have a cat to hug and call her own. The sun had always been too hot, the light too glaring, the neighbours too noisy and low-class. But when Morton was alive she'd told him she loved it, and he seemed to believe her. He certainly had appeared to be happy enough. He'd enjoyed his retirement just the way people were supposed to, and then one day while he was in the garage tinkering with the car, he'd dropped dead of a short, decisive, satisfactorily final heart attack.

The man next door had called the ambulance, his wife had taken her into the house and put her to bed, and before she knew what was happening they'd arranged the funeral and cremation. Since then she had been stranded here exactly like someone washed up on a barren desert island after a catastrophic shipwreck. Nothing else was going to happen until she died, except to watch the man next door kindly cutting her grass and being driven frantic by the noise of his lawnmower.

II

THE EXPATRIATES

It was one of those grey Mediterranean afternoons, when the pines sough autumnally even though it is already March, and thick clouds blowing across the sky threaten rain for days. Jeanette Coleman lay in bed. Terrible, that's how I feel, terrible, her brain throbbed sluggishly and, in obedience to its signals, an arm lifted to the cluttered bed table for the tube of Alka Seltzer and some water. The carafe was empty; the only available liquid a half-glass of stale rum she must have carried upstairs early that morning. Complaining aloud at this negligence, she rang. The single word, 'Water', greeted the maid's appearance. 'Cigarettes,' the hoarse voice added. 'And be quick about it,' she muttered to the closing door, as the girl hurried to the kitchen to warn the others.

She picked up a mirror, looked at herself, then let it drop among the bedclothes. Afternoon light, filtered through the pines, cold and direct from the sea, added years to her thirty-four. But the reflection stiffened her spirit, and she reached for the phone. 'Hello Joe. This is Jeanette. Sure. Listen, have you got something to eat? Good. Send over a cab in half an hour, will you? Good. Thanks.' She relapsed into a reverie in which how terrible the moulded plaster rosettes on the ceiling were, and how terrible she felt, had equal parts, until the maid returned.

'I want a bath,' she said. 'Bath. Get it?' Nodding her head vigorously, the girl went to start it running. Jeanette took an

Alka Seltzer, dragged herself out of bed, and in just under an hour, made-up, dressed, and having drunk the rum and half smoked several cigarettes, was ready to present herself to the world: a small plump blonde with protuberant blue eyes and a sullen mouth, and the arrogant yet uncertain manner of someone who knows that probably the most important factor in any association is that she will be the one to pay the bill.

'Hello, Jeanette,' Joe called as she came through the door with her unsteady walk. 'Sit down.' He was a tall Englishman of forty, who made as much money through various spin-offs of the tourist business as by his bar's high prices. 'What a night!' she said in greeting. 'Why the hell do we drink so much?' Not waiting for a reply, she raised one hand, over which a heavy gold bangle slipped. 'Did you find a bracelet here this morning? Like this, look. I just can't keep a thing. Everything gets lost or stolen.' 'You're too careless, the way you leave things lying around. You can't trust anyone here, I should know,' he answered sententiously. 'You're right about that,' she agreed. 'I was looking through Dick's things yesterday, and half his stuff has gone. Either the maids took it, or that damned male nurse – *practicante*, or whatever they call him. When I first heard that word I thought it meant midwife.'

'How is Dick, anyway?' Joe's voice strained with the effort to sound concerned. 'He's still in that clinic, having shock treatment, and God knows what else done to him, and he can't understand a thing or tell anyone what he wants. It makes me sick to think about it. I would never have brought him here if I'd known this would happen. But he seemed all right.'

Her voice became more unsteady as it rose. 'Tell the waiter to bring a drink, will you? You know what it's like. That damned doctor comes to the house and chatters away, but I still don't know what's happening.' She reached for the glass before the waiter could serve her, and gulped it's contents. The tortured look that had given her face expression for a moment faded. 'I don't know whether to leave him in that clinic, or take him back to the States. What do you think?' The direct question disconcerted Joe. 'The best thing is not to worry. He's being looked after, and he's not able to drink in the clinic, anyway. He must be hell to live with when he's sick. Now relax, and tell me what you want to eat.'

She looked impatiently around the room, and gave a short, hard laugh. Dust under the tables and stains on the upholstery were visible near the unshuttered windows. 'You shouldn't let anyone in here until dark. Or have the place cleaned up. I used to have a bar, back home. You're letting yourself go.' 'I don't know about that,' he said defensively. 'What about that bar idea we were talking about?' He'd clean up, in that sense at least, if he could persuade her to let him be involved.

'I hope it is a good idea. It'll give Dick something to do,' she mused. 'Sometimes he'll pretend he has worked – though he's always had enough money not to need to. Once in a cab he started telling the driver how he'd been a cabby; and with doctors – because his father was a doctor, and he knows the jargon. He'll always try to convince the man he's with that he's done the same job, as if he's ashamed.'

'The bar should make him happy anyway,' Joe steered her back on course. A waiter walked indolently past the table. 'Bring a couple of steaks, will you, Pepe? The most important thing is to get going. I'll be able to leave Pepe in charge here. He's a good barman, and more or less honest.'

But the details of their plan did not interest her at that moment. She was still pushing pieces of charred meat around her plate long after Joe had finished his. Eyebrows contracted and mouth drooping, she began to twist the rings on her large hands. 'For God's sake, Joe! I can't eat this. Don't you have any-thing in the place to drink?' She took a small ampoule from her handbag, shook out a tablet, and held it carefully until the drink came.

It was eight o'clock when Jeanette's taxi pulled up the steep hill and turned into the drive. A strong moist wind whirled her coat open as she walked up the shallow steps. In the darkness the house seemed to lean forward; she had the impression that the elaborate wrought-iron balconies were about to crash down on her head, and the three tall storeys and the tower oppressed with their simultaneous solidity and meaninglessness. Even though she usually liked big houses – everything big appealed to her – this one was too big. But Dick had howled through its rooms, banging on the walls and throwing whatever came to hand. It must be hell in that clinic, she thought, in that tiny room, with his feet hanging off a bed too short for him.

She walked through the dim hall into the living-room, irritated that no one seemed to have heard her enter, then startled for a moment by the seated figure of a plump young man in front of the fire which revealed itself to be the inanely grinning son of the cook. 'What the hell are you doing in here?' she demanded of his retreating, uncomprehending back. She turned on the radio and sat down, avoiding the chair he had vacated. The fire needed more wood, but the basket was empty. Her aimlessness was only aggravated by the need to do the least thing. Instead, she kicked at the half-burnt logs until they collapsed into dully glowing chunks which threw off such heat that she was forced to push back her chair. The music from the radio stopped; she began to pace from one side of the room to the other, observing with jaded eyes the mirror-topped tables and mottled walls, the ostentatious and unused piano, the tasteless wall brackets and bad paintings of the landlord's children; hating this expensive, ugly and inconvenient house. She picked up her coat with the vague hope that somewhere something was happening which might distract her, when one of the doors quietly opened, and a masculine voice, blurred by a strong central European accent said, 'Where are you off to?'

'Oh, Max! I was so damned bored. Go to the kitchen and tell them to bring some wood, will you? And get something to drink.' 'Of course, Jeanette.' He answered like a well-trained major-domo: his position at the hotel where she and Dick had stayed before renting this house.

He returned in a few moments with a tray of bottles, and sat in the armchair opposite. 'How are you feeling today?' For a moment, his expression was one of candid calculation. At twenty-two, he had not yet perfected the art of disguising his thoughts, though as a general rule his features struck exactly the right balance between obsequiousness and arrogance.

'I'm hungry,' Jeanette said. 'I haven't eaten a thing all day.' 'Haven't they cooked?' he asked, indignant and pompous, as if discussing staff at the hotel. 'What would you like?' 'Oh, there should be some cold meat for a sandwich, something like that.' He shook his head, unable to comprehend such lack of interest. The telephone rang. His smooth, multi-lingual voice began a rapid conversation. 'That was the clinic. They say that Dick still wants to leave.' 'Oh God,' she moaned. 'Fix me a drink first, then we can talk about this. I just don't know what to do.' 'Don't worry,' he said, pouring a glass of whisky. He glanced around the room, fearing that his schemes of it might be jeopardised by the too-sudden return of Jeanette's husband. 'Just relax, and I'll go get some food for you. They haven't brought the wood yet, anyway. I'll really have to do something about those people.'

Handing her a plate of sandwiches, he sat down again. A large studio portrait of Dick Coleman stared at him from a side table. It had been taken seventeen years before, when Dick was twenty-three, and Max thought that even then he had looked insane. But to open the conversation, he remarked, 'Dick was very handsome then.' She turned to scrutinise the photograph. 'Yes, that was when we were first supposed to get married. He'd just come back from Europe. He'd gone away after his mother and father were killed by bandits in Central America. Being six years older than me, he seemed terrifically sophisticated. I thought he was wonderful. He was depressed a lot of the time, but we all thought it was natural. Well, the night before the wedding, Dick came over to our place. I was in my room, packing. He sat down and asked me, "Honey, are you happy?" Of course I was, I told him.' Jeanette leaned forward, her gaze so intent that Max, unaware she was looking through him at the remembered scene, did not know what expression to adopt. 'And then – ' she was trying to convey something of the utmost importance now, and stared directly into his eyes ' – he took a gun out of his pocket and said, "I'm happy, too. I'm so happy that I don't think I'll ever be happier. And you're happier than you'll ever be. So I'm going to kill you, and kill myself. There's no point in living any more now."'

She had not told him this part of the story before. 'What did you do?' 'I screamed,' she said drily. 'My mother and father came running in and took Dick downstairs. Of course, we didn't get married – though he was probably right when he said we'd never be so happy again. He went away, and a month later I married someone else.' 'And Dick?' He refilled their glasses. 'Oh, he got married as well. But that only lasted a few weeks, then his wife divorced him and he went into a clinic. My marriage broke up after about three years. I went back home and found him there, living with my parents, and they'd never even told me. My parents and his had been friends all their lives. Well, we did get married, and since then,' she said, her voice swinging bitterly into the present, 'he's been in and out of clinics, more or less as you've seen him. Oh,' she moaned. 'He's so nice sometimes – he seems perfectly all right, and we can have such a good time, and then he'll change . . . and I just don't know what to do.' They had come full circle, and Max's features resumed their normal world-weary expression.

'You'll have to stop worrying,' he said. 'You'll drive yourself crazy, too. You have the best doctors here looking after him.' He built up the dying fire, brought the bottles nearer his chair, and turned on the radio. It was two o'clock in the morning, but he found some late-night dance music. He yawned surreptitiously. After a day at the hotel, these evenings were exhausting. Jeanette would not want to go to bed for hours. Even then, she would have to be coaxed and, like a child, would rather fall asleep in front of the fire than admit the day was finished. And as long as she remained awake she expected him to entertain her. There was really only one sure method of getting her to bed, he thought wryly. But he had convinced himself that his reason for allowing night after night to pass with no more than an occasional embrace was because a direct advance would ruin all his carefully laid plans; and her acceptance of the situation had made him even less confident.

Drunk and tired, he sat on the padded arm of her chair and put a hand on her shoulder. 'Jeanette,' he murmured. 'You're so pretty.' Leaning forward and tentatively kissing her cheek, he was surprised and encouraged when she did not turn away, as sometimes happened. As she lifted her head and met him open-mouthed, though, he felt almost frightened, and pulled back in an attempt to regain his balance. Jeanette rose from the chair with alacrity, so that they were both on their feet at the same moment. She kissed him again and said, 'Sure, let's go to bed.' Slightly dazed, he followed her up the stairs.

Dick Coleman sat at the mirror-topped table in the living-room with a newspaper, a cup and saucer and pot of coffee, and his clean, stiff hands reflected in its silvering depths. It was about ten o'clock, and a clear morning. He had been home from the clinic for five days. A male nurse had come also, but yesterday Dick had thrown him out of the house.

The first day had been wonderful, marred only by Jeanette's refusal to let him have anything to drink. But he was too tired to be seriously annoyed, and by the next morning had already hidden the bottle he bribed a maid to buy. In the afternoon they went for a drive and stopped at just one bar, returning in time for the doctor's visit. Although Dick still felt tired, he was downstairs when Max arrived from the hotel after dinner. Relenting, Jeanette had allowed him a nightcap, unaware he had been sipping from his own supply all day. That final drink almost sent him to sleep, but he had not been

41

entirely insensible, and heard Max murmur something that was disturbing by its very ambiguity. Jeanette hushed him, and bent over Dick's carefully held deception of slumber. Apparently reassured, she nevertheless answered evasively. In a little while Dick came back to life. They sat decorously at opposite sides of the table, drinking and talking softly. He had gone to bed and left them there, and since that evening nothing had happened either to increase or diminish his suspicions.

Although Dick was quite prepared to have Max in the house, to sit and drink and talk with and use as a convenient steward, a sense of his own position revolted at the thought that the young man might be making love to his wife. Knowing that Jeanette was incapable of understanding such a point of view merely increased his mistrust of her. At this moment he only assumed she was in her room; he realised how little he knew of what went on in the house. The expression on his gaunt face was pitiable as he rose to his feet and walked slowly into the hall and up the stairs, still weak from his stay in the clinic, and further debilitated by the sustained effort needed to enact his plan.

Jeanette's room faced him on the first-floor landing. He turned the doorknob quietly. The large bed stretched unruffled between him and the window. Sighing, he withdrew. The next door led to the bathroom, the following to his own quarters. He passed them both, then peered into the dressing-room, but that too was empty. He was now at the end of the hall. On one side a small staircase led up to the attic floor, on the other stood the door of an unused suite. Already he was losing momentum. It seemed as if he had been in the corridor for ever, had opened so many doors that the motive for his search had vanished. About to turn away, his attention was caught by a noise from one of the supposedly vacant rooms.

Without knocking or calling out, he went inside, and before realising what he saw, was halfway across the room. A couple lay on the unmade bed, paralysed by surprise. Two heads were turned to him, four eyes gazed up imploringly. For a moment,

Dick was as unable to move as they. Then all three were released from the spell at the same moment. The man rolled over and sat up, babbling nervously. The girl pulled down her skirt and turned to the wall. Dick recognised the cook's son and one of the maids. He could not understand what the man was saying, and knew that he, also, would not be understood. But as if in explanation, backing away, he said in his high-pitched drawl, 'Sorry, I was just looking for my wife.' He stumbled over the carpet and left the door ajar. Muttering and trembling slightly, he went to his own room to lie down.

It was almost midnight, but they had just finished dinner. Jeanette had delayed the meal until Joe could leave his bar and Max the hotel. 'I talked to the landlord this morning – my God, it was terrible having to see him so early! – and settled about the club. That'll be wonderful, won't it, darling?' She sat on the floor, leaning against Dick's chair, and turned to smile up at him, but his sullen gaze did not leave the fire. In no way disconcerted, she nodded to Joe. 'Yes, I've signed all the papers, and we have it for the season.'

'What are you talking about?' Dick swung his head around sharply. 'We're talking about the nightclub, dear, that you're going to manage this summer. Don't you remember?' 'Oh yes, the nightclub.' His mood changed. 'So you've got it all arranged? Good! I've always said I could manage a place like that. Don't you agree, Joe? I get on well with people, and that's the main thing when you have a bar, isn't it?' He was eager for approval and confirmation, for a long detailed conversation between professional equals.

'Yes, that's the main thing.' Dick's brow wrinkled, trying to gauge Joe's sincerity. Max knew his role. He agreed, while pouring drinks for them all. The doorbell cut into their talk. It sounded as if a large party was entering the house, but Max led in only an elderly British couple, habitués of Joe's bar and permanent members of the foreign colony, and two dandified

Texans, spinning out their post-college Grand Tour. With the shreds of a gracious colonial manner the woman explained that, having met earlier over after-dinner drinks (and presumably boring each other to distraction), they had hit on the alleviating idea of paying the Colemans a visit. The young men could not wait to tell of an adventure earlier that evening. An imperceptive prostitute had tried to pick them up, first singly, then together. 'Bunny,' the woman addressed her husband, a frail-looking man who sat musing over a glass held between mauve-blotched knuckles. 'We'll have to discuss this with the Commandante when we next meet.' 'Yes, of course, dear,' he agreed absently, not lifting his head. 'They've got to live,' Joe said with lazy tolerance.

'This bottle's empty,' Jeanette announced in surprise. 'Is there any more whisky over there?' 'I believe this is brandy I have, my dear,' Bunny murmured. 'Well, there's plenty of that,' Jeanette smiled. 'We're drinking brandy, too,' the others chorused. 'So that means we've finished it on our own. You're not drinking too much, are you, Dick?' 'What do you mean, am I drinking too much?' Dick snapped. 'Do you think I don't know how much I can drink?' 'It's because of what the doctor says – ' Jeanette's eyelids lowered with the modesty of hopelessness. 'I don't want you to get sick again.'

This was the moment of choice, in which he could decide whether to be sane or insane; or so it presented itself to Dick, aware of the muted group hoping he would not sense their dismay. They're watching me as if I'm a dangerous animal, he thought without rancour, and that isn't really how they should look at their host, is it? Of course Jeanette doesn't want me to drink too much, it's because she loves me, isn't it? And these people here, they're really very nice, you don't want to frighten them. No, I don't suppose I do – although of course, it would be fun. It would be terrible, another voice took over, the cracked, desperate voice that remembered the drugs and the shocks, the torturing treatments that scaled him down to skeleton. You wouldn't frighten them as much as they frighten you. Don't let them, then. The earlier, reassuring voice had returned, and he thought this time he would really listen to it. He could feel his resolution, his calmness, distilling more surely every moment, and was glad he had escaped, even if only for a short respite, the terrifying and exhausting necessity to be mad.

'I know, sweetheart, I know,' he muttered. Aware of his swoop away and back to them, Jeanette became intensely animated. 'Where is that drink?' she asked no one in particular, and as if in reply, Max pushed through the door with a bottle of whisky in each hand. 'These are the only two I could find,' he informed her. 'There's enough for now, anyway,' she giggled. But Max's appearance brought back every doubt that Dick had been trying to ignore. The recent effort of self-control left him incapable of another. Two gross birds clamped their talons into the back of his neck, blinding him by the beating of their wings and the scratch of their feathers, choking him with their rank smell, enveloping his head as they strained their necks to reach his eyes. 'Get away!' he cried, flailing long thin arms to drive them off. The glass he was holding dropped to the tiled floor, and surprisingly did not break. 'Get them off me,' he begged. The visitors looked uneasily towards Jeanette, then to Max and Joe, then back again at him. They were embarrassed, curious, and slightly afraid, but Dick felt no pity in them. 'Get them out of here,' he shouted.

'Oh Dick, what's the matter?' Jeanette turned to him in confusion. 'Shall I call the doctor?' Max asked, while the Texans edged away from the group formed by Dick, with Jeanette holding one arm, and Joe ready by his side to grasp the other. 'Get them off me, get them off my head,' Dick screamed again, lunging away from Jeanette with a movement that made those nearest take a step backwards. 'I think it would be best if we went, my dear. Don't bother to show us out,' the Englishwoman said. With an inappropriate smile bestowed impartially on the room, she shut them in and was gone.

'Get hold of the nurse,' Jeanette instructed Max. 'He'll need a shot of something.' Relieved to be out of the eye of the cyclone, Max picked up the phone. 'Come upstairs, sweetheart,' she murmured. 'Come and lie down.' If he lay down, nothing could tear at the back of his neck. Refusing Joe's help, but leaning against Jeanette so heavily that she could barely support his weight, he passed through the hall and up the dimly lit stairs to his room. He was one of the mainstays of the *practicante*'s monthly income, and the man soon arrived on his motorbike to knock Dick out with an injection. He accepted a drink from Jeanette, then left her in front of the fire, talking worriedly to Max and Joe about what to do next.

The beach's gritty margin was littered with evidence that people had been there a short time before, and around the curve of the bay, against the powdery insubstantiality of the foothills in the noon light, newly built hotels could not quite contain the sounds those people made nor the hot oily smell of the meals they were eating. An especially strong gust of frying food reached Dick where he sat in solitary possession. He grimaced with distaste, and moved further away. Bleached cream boxer shorts made his lean body look as dark as an Indian's. Beach life suited him; he sweated out enough alcohol to keep sober. Among the reddening holidaymakers he appeared to be nothing more alarming than a misanthropic and sun-obsessed eccentric. He lay on the stones, stalked regularly back and forth from the bar, sometimes went into the sea, and had not been so healthy for years.

The bar was too big, the rent was too high, and for the sake of the wholesaler's commission, Joe had overstocked it. An evening at the Club Flamingo and a bottle of fizzy wine made a nice change, but the groups of tourists who arrived every fortnight did not come back for a second visit. The dancers danced and the guitarist strummed to the few occupied tables, while from one corner of the room Dick watched sardonically, drank steadily, then more often than not went early to bed.

When Jeanette came, he would put on a shirt and a pair of trousers, and ignore the discussions about business. As far as he was concerned, the pretence she and Joe still maintained about him being in control was a waste of time.

People were coming back, mostly the young and energetic who did not take wine at lunch or need a siesta. Although the sun was high they wanted to shout and throw balls to each other, and there was always a couple pumping their legs up and down on a *pedalo*. Their return signalled that it was time for Dick to eat, and he started across the road to the bar. Almost there, he saw a figure which immediately put him on guard. Dressed in a pair of white trousers pressed into military perfection, and a brass-buttoned blazer more elegant than worn by any client of the hotel where he worked, Max sat in the shade of the doorway – meaning that Jeanette was present on one of her tours of inspection. Instead of the dark peace of the sun he would be in the confusing gloom of the bar in daylight; the familiar emptiness of his existence was going to be filled with talk and people.

'Here comes the manager.' Max grinned over his shoulder towards Jeanette and Joe, talking inside. Jeanette smiled distractedly. The overstocking had made her angry, but now crates of drink were missing, and it was obvious that Joe had taken them to his own bar. The two waiters, eating at an empty table, listened indifferently to their tense voices. Dick ignored the others and greeted his wife. By comparison to the firm tanned bodies of the girls who ran up and down the beach all day, she looked pale and tired. Her light dress was creased from the drive and her skin damp from the heat. He wondered why she was getting thinner. 'You look well, Dick,' she said. Strolling over from the doorway, Max added, 'This life of responsibility suits him.' 'Yes, it does suit me,' Dick responded aggressively. 'Let's have a drink, Joe. Come on, all of you, have it on me. Have it on the house.'

They sat down. No one mentioned lunch. They were glad to remain silent and listen to Dick's anecdotes of beach life, lulled by the afternoon shadows and his apparent stability into not realising how much he was drinking.

A gesture of Max's changed everything. Dick reared up from his chair. 'How dare you come here with my wife, wearing those trousers!' Uncomprehending, they watched him pour his drink over Max's legs, then scoop all glasses from the table and hurl them to the floor. His thin, dark body seemed barely human as he leaped over the bar and plucked bottles from the shelves, then threw them in all directions. The waiters withdrew rapidly, as did Max, furious about his ruined clothes. Dick cursed them all – the birds at his neck that would not leave him alone, the insult of the white trousers – until the place was wrecked. Limbs and torso slippery with sweat and bloody from the broken glass, by then he was exhausted. Jeanette crouched on the wet floor and held his head close to her breast.

Their voices brought her to the top of the stairs. Max was talking to the cook's son. 'How are you getting on with Catalina?' The boy giggled proudly. 'You'd better not stain those mattresses,' Max poked him in the side. 'You're the lucky one, having a nice young girl like that. She looks the loving type, eh?' The phone rang from a nearby room, but neither moved. Jeanette called, 'Max, answer the phone.' 'It's probably only the clinic.' She picked up his irritable undertone and, afraid he would not pay attention to what was said, clattered downstairs to take the call herself. The daily report on Dick's condition was the same: no change. A new treatment kept him subdued, and he had even gained weight. He no longer complained about the food or his bed when she went to see him; he had nothing to say at all. 'I suppose he's improving,' Max said. 'Do you want him to get worse, and die?' 'Good God, no. Do you think I want to be stuck with you?' 'I'm not that much of a fool,' she answered bitterly. He must have thought better of what he was about to add, for he stopped, then continued in an entirely different tone. 'Don't be angry, sweetheart. I know

48

it always makes you nervous when you hear from the clinic. Let's have a drink, or do you want to go out?' 'What do you want?' She smiled and touched his shoulder. 'Do you feel like going out?' Masterfully, he opted for an evening at home.

'Let's have a party,' he suggested after the first drink. Jeanette did not respond with the enthusiasm she might have shown the previous spring. Since Max had moved in, she thought there had been far too many parties. 'We can't just sit here staring at each other,' he said in a menacing tone. 'Sure, sure, good idea,' she hastily agreed. 'Who do you want to phone?' His suggested list of guests included Joe. 'No, I won't have him here,' she stated firmly. 'You know that. Why do you keep trying?'

The season ended before the Bar Flamingo had covered the costs of its opening. Their final accounting revealed that Joe had cheated her even more than allowed for. She wanted to break the association completely, but Max refused. 'I have business of my own with him.' 'But he really cheated me,' she said. 'Don't you understand? I hate the bastard.' 'It doesn't matter,' he replied. 'I've still got to keep on good terms with him.' He declined to explain, but from time to time asserted his power by sitting her on a stool at Joe's bar while he and Joe retired to a back room to do whatever it was their business involved.

'All right, then. I won't phone Joe. There'll be enough people anyway.' 'This place is a mess, with all these parties,' she remarked. 'Well, why don't you have it cleaned up?' Max had given up his supervision of the domestic staff, but Jeanette's previous slight authority had been entirely undermined when he moved into the house. The only work that seemed to go on was the preparation of elaborate meals for the servants, and the provisioning this involved. Occasionally two plates of food got as far as the dining-room, though more often Jeanette found herself grubbing in a larder of left-overs, the remains of meals she had never seen, smelt or tasted; slicing the ends of what had been large joints of meat in order to make a few sandwiches. But in the chaotic melancholy of her daily life, the horrendous bills seemed too unimportant to concern her. Everything needed cleaning. Even Max's room was filthy – she had learned that his impeccable appearance bore no relationship to the setting in which it was achieved. Apart from the food which the servants took home, linen and clothes disappeared. When Dick went back to the clinic she had put his things away, but half the dirty shirts upstairs belonged to him: worn by Max and then pushed into the bottom of his closet – or perhaps by the cook's son, she had no way of knowing. That afternoon she had spent almost an hour looking for a favourite blouse. The search had been unsuccessful. Like bracelets, brassières, Dick's winter overcoat, and her own ideas about the future, it had vanished.

Max and Joe's business was currency. Jeanette knew that Max could get her a better rate than anyone else, but was not aware of Joe's part in these transactions. Most of Dick's income was consumed by medical expenses, but Jeanette's mother had left her enough investments to live even at the present level. Cheques arrived at three-monthly intervals. At Max's suggestion, the last two had been sent direct to her rather than through a bank. He returned them in the form of thick piles of soft, creased notes that seemed to have no connection to the thin slip of paper he had taken away; the spending of which could never be a serious matter. She offered him the current cheque. 'It's a bit tricky right now,' he said. 'Keep it for a few days.'

It was larger than the others, and getting hold of so much currency would not be easy. But Max wanted to feel absolutely certain that the critical moment had arrived, when hesitation would only result in fatal regret. He could remain in his present job, or get another at any hotel in the world. But with so much money, everything could be different. The memory of how he had allowed Jeanette to lead him to her bed made him gloat at the prospect.

If he could manage without Joe being aware that he had gone until hearing it as a piece of gossip days later – so much the better. Joe had always been too condescending, joked too often about his eager and badly concealed ambitions. Joe might betray him, or demand some of Jeanette's money in exchange for silence. After weighing up the advantages of various methods, Max decided to put the cheque into his Swiss bank account, and use his own funds as cash in hand.

He was surprised by how sentimental he felt, once he was sure what to do. He might even miss Jeanette. But she had become too melancholy, a sadness not caused by him and therefore belittling; good reason to abandon her. This swindle would strip away the final shreds of what had captivated him. By the time everything was settled in his own mind, Jeanette's cheque had been deposited, his savings converted into francs and dollars, and his travelling wardrobe (which included some items of Dick's) conveyed out of the house. He would have liked to say something to serve as a farewell, a few sentences whose significance would only be understood later. But nothing sufficiently allusive occurred to him; he was afraid to give himself away. He left the house one morning when Jeanette was asleep, collected a month's salary and, giddy with fear and excitement, took a cab for the airport.

The storms that autumn went on and on; starting the day Max left, they seemed to become worse as she realised what had happened, then settle into a steady, downpouring monotony. Apart from her daily visit to the clinic, she did not leave the house, but sat in the poorly lit salon before an ineffectual fire drinking slowly through bottle after bottle of whatever was brought. For three days she made no move to find Max, so that when she did contact the police, he had successfully vanished. She wrote to her brokers for more money, and settled back into lethargic indifference. Then one morning she woke to the shock of a clear sky, colour and light and shadows again.

As she left Dick's room, a nurse asked Jeanette if she had time to see the director. 'Your husband seems to be in a calm phase. If nothing disturbs him it should continue. Do you intend to remain in this city?' His direct question made her realise that she had no plans at all. The events of the year marshalled themselves into high walls that diminished backwards and led forward to embarkation. 'My husband's illness has kept me here longer than intended. If I thought he could travel – ' 'You must know about his illness by now,' the man answered, pushing one sidepiece of his glasses back as they spoke, as if it were a childhood habit never lost. 'No one can say when he will become really ill again. He is not a well person, nor will he ever be. But I think you could travel with him. If you did it slowly, he might enjoy it.' 'I prefer to fly,' she mused. 'But there'll be a lot of luggage – it would probably be better to take the boat. When can he leave?' 'Whenever you wish, Madame.' He pushed the glasses up his nose again, his voice colder. 'Well, he can come with me now.' She would be glad to have Dick back home, whatever this severe-looking man might think.

When the house was cleared of what she had bought in attempts to make it more comfortable, the damage to walls and furniture was exposed. One sunny morning she went over it with the agent while he listed the repairs and replacements to be made. His experience of renting furnished houses to foreigners led him to expect arguments about each separate item, and he was disappointed to be deprived of one of the more subtle gratifications of the job.

The cook, the cook's son, and the two maids were as emotional as old family retainers as she distributed parting bonuses. Tall and ghostly, Dick echoed her farewells. Jeanette also was pale as they entered the taxi; it had been hard work, arranging their departure. She had drunk too much and not slept enough and had lost more weight. Her face looked slacker and older. All the bars were illuminated as they drove past them on the way to the night ferry, and through the misted windows she thought she saw those people who had come to her many parties. At the quay it was raining again, and she took Dick's arm as they shuffled up the gangplank on to the boat.

SOIR DE FÊTE

i   The Mirrors

It was almost dark. Sunset sea-wind tapped the bedroom blind against the side of the open balcony door, and lights from the apartments opposite and noise from the café three floors below emphasised the general excitement. A burst of laughter sounded as loud as if in the same room. They looked at each other, startled; then Charles gave an answering laugh, as though he too had heard the joke. While Betty fastened her bracelets and Ann adjusted a sandal, he slowly pivoted in front of the long mirror, studying his posture with sad dark eyes. At nearly fifty, his body was that of an athletic young man. It was only when he was trapped into discussion of abstract matters that his face lost the confident expression formed by years of commercial success.

'Let's have a drink before we go.' The direct glare of an over-head light accentuated every line and hollow of Betty's face, changing an attractive blonde of forty-five into an old woman. Sensing the unfortunate contrast to the dark girl half her age, she turned away to kiss Ann's shoulder.

Ann had met Charles and Betty the week before, at a café on the promenade. They personified every reason for abandoning friends, family and job, yet she was glad to be with them and postpone from day to day the realisation of how lost she felt on this continent where no one knew of her existence. Lurking at the back of her mind were justifying precedents of patronage, and the relative position of rich shopkeepers and ambitious young artists. When they suggested she share their newly rented apartment she had moved in that same morning, *Quinze Août.*

After the toast, there seemed nothing to say. Flashes of light from the tilted wineglasses were repeated from moving eyes furtively assessing each other, the crumpled shimmer of Betty's nightdress on a padded chair and the large mirror in which they were pinkly reflected. Charles sighed, licking his lips. His glass clinked against the glass-topped dressing table as he put it down to touch Ann's arm and ask, 'Well, are you enjoying yourself?'

'What a question!' Betty glared at him. 'Of course you're enjoying yourself, aren't you, darling? Doesn't she look pretty, Charles? But I think she needs something around her neck.' Her tone of voice implied a cue.

Turning to view the effect of Betty's borrowed blouse, Ann sounded dubious. 'I think it's fine like this.'

'Go on,' Betty murmured to her husband.

Like a magician at the successful climax of a trick, Charles displayed a two-stranded pearl necklace between outraised hands. But glancing over her shoulder, Ann carelessly said, 'No thanks, that's not right,' then picked up a tube of lipstick and peered into the mirror.

Puffs of air eddied through the slats of the blind as more people passed along the street below. Charles held the necklace out again. Seeing he would receive no help from Betty, he said weakly, 'Look, Ann. Don't you think it's nice?'

Her face, reflected in the mirror, was enough to send Charles sauntering into the corridor, where he began to whistle. When she saw that Ann's flush had faded, Betty began. 'I didn't know you were so silly. If a man wants to give you a present, you should accept it. You've only made Charles feel a fool.'

'I didn't know it was supposed to be a present. I thought it was yours, or something – ' she ended lamely.

'Why would he lend you my necklace?' Betty asked, her voice scornful. 'You were just stupid. Now go and say you've changed your mind.'

'I can't do that!'

'Don't be so silly. You need some pretty things. You'll be glad to have it, one day. And you'll make Charles happy, too. I should know him by now, we've been married more than twenty years. Now go on, do as I tell you.' She pushed her towards the door.

Ann turned for support to her reflection in the corridor mirror, trying to imagine it with the addition of the necklace. But what was going to happen between this moment and that was so hard to accept that she was tempted to run down into the street and never see them again. Behind her own reversed image appeared that of Betty's eyes. Resigning herself, she tapped on the door of Charles's room.

'Why don't you come in?' The necklace gleamed in the light from his desk lamp.

'I guess I do need something to wear around my neck, after all,' she blurted out.

'I hoped you'd like it.' He sounded relieved. 'Let me fasten the clasp.'

Through the thin cloth she felt the beads' weight and coldness. He put an arm round her shoulders and swung them both around to face the door. 'Doesn't she look fine?' he asked as his wife entered the room, already smiling.

'Very pretty.' Kissing Ann, she whispered, 'Now, isn't that better?'

'Let's get going,' Charles's voice was as enthusiastic as a boy's. In the corridor he stopped in front of the hall mirror with Ann to comment on what a handsome pair they made.

'Be sure to lock the door,' Betty said, as they stepped into the brightly lit cage of the elevator and descended to the carnival.

ii The Confetti

The promenade had been blocked off. Near the paybox, men were selling confetti. While Betty waited in line for entry tickets, Charles bought three bags of the largest size. In the movement and glitter and din of the hot night it was almost impossible to remember that a cool indifferent sea lapped against the shore, only yards away.

Elated and restless, they prowled the narrow pathway left between spectators' backs and hotel terrace walls, hardly aware of the passing procession except where the line of watchers thinned to show a float bearing a group of girls in one sort of costume or other – now flowers, now pierrots, now slaves in an Eastern market with arms held by the wrist to a pole and looking as uncomfortable as if they really were slaves, yet smiling down at the crowd. Charles pranced ahead with three new bags gripped under one arm, hurling it into the face of anyone who caught his eye.

'Let me have some more. Look, mine's all finished.' Panting with laughter, Betty ran towards him.

His response was to empty an entire bag of it over her head. 'You bastard!' She pushed him away with one hand, brushing her hair and dress with the other, and spitting the bits stuck to her lips at his face. He put an arm roughly around her shoulders and said, 'Keep quiet, here's another bag,' then hurried ahead.

'Look what that pig has done,' Betty complained when Ann caught up with her. 'Let's give him the same.'

The road was almost deserted near the end of the promenade, where they found Charles and dragged him into the shallow curve of a gateway. Betty laughed, and sprinkled a few disks of confetti over his head in token of triumph, but Ann threw her handful directly into his face. Shaking his head, he charged forward. For a few minutes he could not catch her. But she was trapped by the high wall of a villa. Pressing her against it with his strong body, he systematically poured confetti into her hair and

58

down the front of her blouse, smeared it into her face, and did not stop until the bag was empty. Several passers-by halted, interested or censorious, but no one interfered until Betty arrived.

'Leave her alone!' Charles stared blankly for a moment, then abruptly stopped laughing. When Ann had spat the last of the dry, sour powderiness from her mouth he had disappeared.

'He doesn't know when to stop.' Betty said. 'Are you all right, darling?' Ann made no reply except to take Betty's arm. But soon their linked hands dropped apart, and they were laughing as loudly as everyone else.

A group of three young men in leather jackets began to circle round them, speaking a language neither could understand. Betty's tanned face and gold jewellery glittered in the light of the decorated street lamps as she swaggered along, delighted by their attentions. One of the men drew closer, as if enthralled.

Ann caught sight of Charles a few yards ahead, a half-empty bag of confetti in one hand, and pushed towards him. At that moment the young man grasped Betty's arm. She shrugged away and joined them with an expression of relief, gasping, 'He was beginning to get on my nerves.'

With every step the crowd thickened until it was impossible to move in any direction. Voices and music could be heard from the hotel terrace behind, but there was little speech from this group, whose efforts to churn a way forward only made the situation worse.

'Are you OK?' Charles pulled Ann around, and saw the fear in her dilated eyes. He kept hold of her arm, and said, 'We'd better stay put until they start moving again.' A woman screamed nearby. An answering cry burst from Ann's throat.

Behind the picket fence was a hedge of the same height, and behind that the stone wall of a hotel terrace. The thin wooden palings and thorny bushes bent backwards as the pressure grew. Turning to grasp the top of the fence before she lost her balance, Ann's fingers were crushed against the stones. She screamed again; Charles scrambled on to the top of the wall and dragged her up to him, then reached for Betty.

They were on the terrace of a grand hotel, whose guests stared with surprise at these creatures who had irrupted upon them. They sat down at an empty table, and Ann laughed tremulously. 'Imagine acting like that!'

'Try to keep calm, otherwise you'll get hurt,' Betty admonished. 'You're all right now, aren't you?'

'Sure, she's all right,' Charles said dismissively. 'Why doesn't a waiter come over? This place is no damned good, anyway,' he muttered after ten minutes, and brusquely led them through the lobby and into the street.

At the first bar they stopped for a drink. A glass of brandy on top of the wine they had shared before leaving the apartment was far more than Charles's normal intake. He leaned forward to pat Ann's face. His was covered with sweat, and she thought he looked quite drunk. 'You're having a good time, aren't you, honey? You like Betty and me, don't you? We'll give you a good time.'

'Come on, you old fool,' Betty interrupted. 'We'll miss the fireworks if we don't get going.'

iii   The Stones

Through dim, confusing beams of light from the promenade, the moon and the sea, they stumbled across the sloping beach of smooth oval stones.

Haven't we come too far?' Ann wondered, but Betty insisted that the further they went, the better the view would be. At last she came to a halt by the sea wall and sat down in its shadow. She tugged at Ann's arm to pull the girl down to her side, while Charles pressed close on the other. Ann leaned back, uncomfortable, feeling the heat from their bodies and smelling the drink on their breath. With a sound like a piece of silk being violently ripped, the first firework arched across the sky.

A bursting rocket shivered a highlight along the bottle in Charles's hand. 'I bought this at the bar,' he explained, putting an arm round her shoulders. 'Have a drink.'

Ashamed of her loss of control and eager to make them forget it, Ann accepted a sip of the brandy.

'Don't hog it all.' Betty slid a hand across her wrist like a warm shackle. 'Give me some, honey.'

'Loosen up, sweetheart,' Charles slurred as the bottle went round again. 'We'll all have a good time.'

'Sure, we'll all have a good time,' Betty echoed.

Plumes of light sifted across the sky and paled the sea for a moment as they dissolved into its blackness.

'Why don't you get comfortable? Come on, here, a bit closer to me.' Charles dragged Ann's head against his shoulder and began to fumble at her clothes. Pushing his hands away, she heard Betty's voice, bizarrely polite, as though offering a plate of cakes, say, 'Go on, don't be shy. I won't mind.'

On the empty beach, she felt a recurrence of the choking fear that had mastered her in the thick of the crowd, and the impulse which had made her want to run out of their apartment. Pushed against the stony wall and the stones of the beach, she tried to move away, but as the treacherous pebbles shifted, only seemed to dig herself in deeper. Fireworks surged above the town and rained down into the sea, alternately obscuring and revealing two intent faces.

'What's the matter with you?' Charles snapped. 'What're you so nervous for? You're a big girl, you know what it's all about.' He emphasised his words by pressing her down on to the stones.

'Don't be such a baby,' Betty added. 'We only want to enjoy ourselves and for you to enjoy yourself, too. There's no harm in it.' She began to stroke one of Ann's knees.

'Sure, we can have a lot of fun.' Charles was tugging at her briefs. 'Just be a good girl and see how much you like it.'

'I don't want to.' It was hard to articulate the words now that his mouth writhed against hers.

'Listen to her!' Charles proclaimed to the entire night sky. 'I thought she was so broad-minded!'

Betty tried to quieten him, and his hold relaxed. The moment she became aware of this, Ann attempted to stand up, but in immediate response, Charles crashed her down with a blow from his elbow. The hopelessness of her position now emphasised by the regular, indifferent rise and fall of the elaborate set-pieces heralding the finale, Ann shouted for help.

'For God's sake, keep quiet.' Betty clapped a hand over Ann's mouth, then snatched it away. 'The little bitch! She bit my hand!'

'I'll keep her quiet,' Charles said. 'Here, hold her legs.'

'Be careful,' Betty remarked, sliding round to take his place.

'She's biting me, too,' he said in drunken amazement. 'She sure is wild. But all the better. She should calm down in a few minutes and then we can talk some sense.'

'Don't press too hard,' Betty warned jokingly.

An enormous illumination filled the sky, and they both turned to watch. It was some minutes until the last firework blossomed, spread and faded, and left them in a darkness in which they could barely see. Bending towards Ann again, Charles remarked, 'She seems OK now.'

'Are you feeling better, sweetheart?' Betty asked, loosening her hold. 'Take your hand away,' she advised. 'She probably can't talk.' Betty leaned closer. Blinded by the fireworks, she was not sure of what she saw. She began to shake Ann's shoulder.

'What's the matter?' They stared at each other in the dim light, eyes glowing with fear. 'I couldn't have!' he answered the unspoken question. When Betty lifted Ann's head it rolled loosely, then dropped back when she released it, the pearl necklace clinking against the stones.

Everything was silent as if the whole town were still dazed by the display. But even as they listened they could hear the shuffling of dispersal and the rising volume of voices. Betty stood up and tugged at Charles's hand. 'We've got to get away.'

He gazed down at the figure on the stones. 'I told you it was crazy to bring her to the beach. None of your ideas is ever any good.'

'Let's go,' Betty hissed. She dragged him to his feet then hurried to the first set of wooden steps up to the promenade. 'Hurry Charles,' she implored. She scanned the crowd in each direction but no one took any interest in another drunken middle-aged couple leaving the fête.

PLEASURE

'You're so stupid,' Eric laughed. 'Yes, you're really a stupid girl. Why don't you stop talking and have another drink?' Phyllis looked up with vague, hurt eyes. 'Why do you trouble to answer, if I'm so stupid?' she slurred in an exaggeratedly genteel tone of voice, then dropped her blonde head with a heavy movement towards the glass in her hand. She was even more drunk than he. Alchohol had made her pedantic, dizzy and easily hurt, while its effect on him was to intensify all his febrile aggression.

'Isn't she a stupid girl?' He was a thin, nervous man of thirty-eight, with a malicious face and long, smooth brown hair. Tilting his chair until he could put an arm around the girl seated at each side, he shook them irritably and demanded again, 'Isn't Phyllis a stupid girl?'

They smiled noncommittally. The six of them were sitting at the one occupied table in the club. It was long past closing time; all lights but those over the bar had been switched off, the piano was shut, and except for a garrulous old man swearing earnestly as he explained something to the barmaid, they were the only customers. The proprietor was trying to ease them out and close for the night.

'Let's have another drink,' Eric called. 'All right, Siddy?' Siddy wearily agreed, and another round was served. As soon as he had gulped down his Scotch, Eric began again.

'You finished that one quickly. Didn't she finish it quickly,

65

Peter?' He turned to the man opposite. His clothes were grey, his hair was grey, and his skin was grey. Only his eyes showed a touch of colour; bloodshot, frantic eyes that jarred with the placatory drawl of his reply, as he glanced from mistress to business partner, as if afraid she could become the cause of a costly disagreement. 'Why don't you leave her alone, Eric?'

But jumping up from the seat, Eric pulled out his jacket lapels to indicate a bosom, and minced around the table with a partridge hobble, calling out in a high affected voice, 'Look at me, I'm Phyllis.' Even Peter became breathless with amusement, while Phyllis sat with the full mouth Eric had mimicked so well set in an unhappy pout, protuberant blue eyes bewildered and resentful.

Swaying past her chair, Eric snatched the combs from her hair and pushed it forward over her face. Emphasising each word, he pronounced, 'Now Phyllis's hair is untidy, and no one will love her. Doesn't she look silly? You don't love her any more, do you, Peter? No, no one loves Phyllis.'

Listlessly she smoothed back a tress, then looked up like a child who does not know whether to believe what it is told. 'What a stupid face!' Eric was disgusted by such vulnerability. 'But I've got your combs,' he taunted. 'And you can't have them back!' He danced a few paces into the room, his grin overlying a strained watchfulness, wanting to make sure they were all paying attention.

Siddy switched off another light. The heavy pleats in one of the girls' skirts suddenly flattened, a mirror on the other side of the room disappeared, and glasses stacked on the bar ready for next day's drinking seemed about to dissolve as they lost the streaked hardness the light had given them. Siddy coughed meaningfully. 'Don't you all want to go home?'

'We'll be off in a minute, don't worry,' Eric assured him. 'Let's have one more drink first.' He turned back to Phyllis. 'Why is your hair all over your face? Why are you so untidy? Look at you!' He drew her unprotestingly towards the mirror behind the bar.

The slack, bad-complexioned face of a slender girl in her mid-twenties shone palely back, lipstick worn off except for a thin hard outline. A piece of torn lace hung from the edge of one sleeve, her black suede evening shoes were stained, and she wore no stockings. By contrast, Eric was immaculate in white shirt and fine Prince of Wales check suit.

'You'd better stop all this drinking, you know, and running after him.' He jerked his head to indicate the dark young man talking to Peter. 'Peter will drop you if you don't. Why don't you get him to marry you?'

'I'm not running after Jerry,' she protested. 'It's not true!'

'Yes you are. I know you're in love with him.'

'I'm not! I'm in love with Peter. He's very sweet.'

'My God,' said Eric. 'If any woman said I was very sweet, I'd kick her teeth in.'

She stared with wide-open eyes, wondering what she had said wrong. Unable to find an answer, she slid off the barstool and approached Peter with unsteady steps. 'He's got my combs. Make him give them to me.'

'Now darling,' he murmured. 'It's only a joke.' He patted her shoulder soothingly, but she pulled away and with arms akimbo loudly reiterated the demand.

Looking as if someone had drawn a skull in sooty lines on his fat face, Siddy padded over and also attempted to calm her. But she backed further into the shadowy room, only a few folds of crimson skirt and her glaring eyes catching the light. 'I want my combs!' she shouted, open-mouthed but otherwise ominously rigid. Peter hurried over. 'All right, sweetheart, I'll get the combs,' he promised. 'Just sit down, and I'll bring them to you.'

At this assurance, she allowed herself to be led back to the table, where she slumped into a chair and stared dully at the stained, wet top. The two girls – neither of whom would have dared to make such a scene – thinking that she was too drunk to notice, observed her with a mixture of awe and distaste, but Phyllis suddenly rounded on them. 'Why are you staring at me?

Why don't you get drunk, and behave properly in the circumstances? You're nothing but fools!'

'Now, Phyllis,' Eric said in an amused tone, behind her. 'Don't be rude.' He laid a hand on her shoulder, but she jumped up and spat out, 'Don't touch me! And give me back my combs!'

Head cocked to one side, he smiled wanly, as if beginning to be bored with the whole thing. 'Peter has them.' He sat down and absent-mindedly began to play with a hand of one of the girls.

'Here are your combs, darling,' Peter murmured, hoping she would take them without comment. She did not notice the spasm of hatred that crossed Eric's face as she pushed them back into her hair with a triumphant grimace.

'Phyllis is in love with Jerry,' he announced. 'Isn't that so, Phyllis? Aren't you in love with Jerry? Come on, you might as well admit it, everyone knows you're in love with him.'

The dapper Jerry diplomatically looked away.

'How dare you say such a thing?' she spluttered.

'Don't be such a stupid woman,' he snapped back.

'She doesn't really love Jerry,' Peter interposed in an apprehensive voice, longing for peace. 'Do you, darling?'

'What a perfectly ridiculous question! You know he's only trying to make trouble between us.'

'Well,' Eric sighed, dropping the matter. 'We should let Siddy go to bed. Come on, everyone.' He helped the girls on with their coats, then gently guided them through the hall and out into the cold night.

The wind attacked their throats and nostrils, and lifted them to a more extreme degree of drunkenness. Huddled at the top of the steps, they peered dubiously into vague blackness smudged, like faint chalky marks on a sheet of dark grey paper, by the road, empty but for Eric's Bentley, and the dim houses opposite.

'Get in the car,' Eric commanded. 'We'll go to Peter's place. It's far too soon to go to bed. Bed is where you die.'

Peter and the girls slid obediently into the back, and Jerry took the front passenger seat.

'Come on, Phyllis,' Eric laughed. 'Look, you can sit on Jerry's lap.' He was delighted by his own mischief.

'Shut up,' she hissed. 'I won't get into your car. I'm going to walk home.'

'Don't be such a silly woman.' Afraid she might elude him, Eric spoke with a pretence of good humour.

'I do like to walk sometimes, you know.'

'Come into the car, Phyllis.' Peter added his persuasions, peering from the side window.

'No, I'm walking,' she repeated, and took a few steps, clutching her coat close.

'Oh, let her go,' Peter said, settling into his corner. 'The walk will do her good.'

Eric ignored him, and slid the car slowly along the pavement until he was abreast of Phyllis. 'Don't be silly, get in.'

'I prefer to walk.'

'You know I want you to come in,' he cajoled. 'It's too cold out there for you.' The large lighted vehicle was like a phosphorescent animal stalking her. 'Silly Philly, silly Philly,' Eric cackled from his open window.

The wind whirled her soft hair upwards as she turned away, and twisted the heavy coat around her legs so that she stumbled.

'Come inside to pretty Jerry. He still has his suntan, did you know that?'

'Stop it!' she shouted, running towards the car, arms lifted as if she would have liked to destroy it.

With a vicious grinding of gears and brakes, he pulled it up on to the pavement, blocking her way.

'Come on in, darling, don't be silly,' Peter called anxiously.

She pushed between the fenders and the wall and hurried on. Passing beneath a street lamp that gilded her head, she looked like a panic-stricken moth.

Cursing, Eric reversed, then the car jumped forward and was

level with her. 'Are you getting in?' he spat out. When she did not answer, he mounted the pavement once more, but again she squeezed by and hurried down the street, her face flushed, excited and triumphant.

The four passengers sat tense and dumb, dreading an accident.

'She's doesn't want to be ordered about,' Peter protested. 'We're nearly there. Let her walk the rest of the way.'

'The silly bitch is going to do what I say,' was Eric's response, as he manoeuvred the car forward again.

The lamps hung over the road rocked in the wind, arcs of light and shadow intersecting and separating like a kaleido-scope. Along its wide, straight length they were the only people awake and moving.

It seemed a long time before they caught up with her, arrogant on high, fragile heels.

'Are you getting in?' Eric called menacing.

There was no answer.

They each knew what was going to happen, and even she stood still, waiting for the ritual re-enactment. And because they knew it, their concentration wavered. Before anyone realised, the mudguard of the near wheel had hit her leg.

'You murderer!' she screamed.

'For God's sake, Eric, what have you done?' Peter shouted, pushing across the girls to open the door.

'She's all right.' Eric's tone expressed only indifference.

The two girls looked into each other's eyes and drew closer together.

When the door opened once more, and Peter helped Phyllis into the back of the car, Eric nonchalantly said, 'Oh, so you decided to come in after all, did you?'

Nursing her bruised leg, she made no reply.

No one spoke until the car stopped. As if nothing unusual had happened, Eric ushered them out and remarked, 'Well, I could do with a drink.'

Phyllis hobbled towards a pale brocade-covered couch and

lay down, while Peter crossed to the cocktail cabinet and began organising drinks. The others followed into the untidy, high-ceilinged, cigarette-stale drawing room. Quite soon, when Eric – who until then had ignored her – sat in a nearby chair and said, 'Easy enough to have him pour out a glass of whisky. Why don't you prove you really love me, and make a pot of tea?' Phyllis smiled back. It was an old joke between them.

III

ANOTHER SURVIVOR

He's fifty now, but the day his mother and father took him to the railway station with the one permitted suitcase, clutching a satchel crammed with entomological collecting equipment he refused to leave behind – that chilly, too harshly bright day of a windy reluctant spring – was in 1938, and he was twelve years old. With the other children lucky enough to be part of this refugee group on its way to England, and their agitated and mournful parents, they moved to the far end of the platform in an attempt to make themselves less conspicuous. Rudi recognised two of the boys from last year at school. Since the holidays he had been kept at home.

A few children had begun to cry, unable not to respond to the tears their parents tried so hard to repress. The entire group emanated a collective desolation, unaffected by any individual attempt to put a good face on matters, or hopeful talk of future reunion. For all of them, as the adults already suspected, it was to be their last sight of each other. Sharing a stridently upholstered couch with three men as withdrawn into their separate worlds as he is, staring unseeingly at other patients moving restlessly around the crowded day-ward, Rudi's face is still marked by the same appalled expression which had settled on it that morning.

His parents belonged to families that had lived in the city for generations. Though Rudi was an only child, there had been many houses and apartments where he was at home, many celebrations to attend and cousins to play with. The family ramified through the professions: doctors, lawyers, architects, academics – part of that cultivated, free-thinking flowering of Jewish emancipation whose crucial importance to the European spirit only became apparent after its destruction. His father had been a biologist, his mother a talented amateur pianist. At night, in the dormitory of the school he was sent to by the same kindly people who sponsored his rescue, he tried to fall asleep by reconstructing themes from the music she had played. He remembered creeping up behind her, steps deadened by soft Persian rugs whose silk nap glinted in the mote-laden beams of afternoon sunlight filtered through creamy lace curtains, hoping to reach the piano and put his hands over her eyes before she even realised he was home from school.

That was the most precious image on the iconostasis of memory during the years when there was no news of them at all. That, and another one, from a Sunday country walk with his father. Even now, through the distractions of hospital life, he can relive the surge of pride and intellectual excitement that came when he finally understood his father's explanation why the hills had their particular structure and composition: a lesson in geography and geology; remember also how he had called upon that memory to sustain him through every boyhood crisis.

Though he mastered English quickly and did his schoolwork well, the prospect of taking part in the war and adding his energy to the fight against Nazism was what obsessed him. But he had not even crossed the Channel before it ended. And then, after seven years of suspense, of great swoops between hope and an absolute conviction that his parents had vanished, the camps were opened up and the first reports and pictures began to appear. The effort he makes, even now, is to shut off parts of his mind, to push all that information away. Nightmares, day-mares – black, white, bleeding, disembowelled, flayed: Goya-esque mares with staring, maddened eyes had been galloping across the wincing terrain of his brain ever since. Yet he was unable to stop accumulating the facts; nor stop imagining that every atrocity heard or read about had been suffered by his parents.

Then he calmed down, came through: another survivor. So much time passed that he could even acknowledge how privileged and fortunate he was, weighed in the balance of the global misery. Every morning he could read in the newspapers stories of war, famine, torture and injustice, and recognise that he was no more affected than the newspaper-readers of that past time had been by reports of the catastrophe which engulfed his family. He was healthy, prosperous, successful. His wife had not left him. His children were growing up. His work presented no real problems. It was just that now, after more than thirty years, he was overcome with the most intense yearning for his mother. He still felt like a boy of twelve, gone away from home for the first time: the adoring son of a proud, doting mother who cannot be diverted by promises of even the most fabulous pleasures if they will keep him away from his mother one moment longer. And the strength of this need made him aware of how much grief had been repressed when they parted.

For the first time, he could remember his mother before the war began. Since their separation, he had only been able to imagine her as a victim, not a woman at the height of her vigour and self-confidence. During the intervening years, memory had been blotted out by imagination, always the stronger.

Twenty years ago when Rudi and Barbara bought their house, the streets between Camden Town and Primrose Hill were neither fashionable nor expensive. They had lived there ever since, while houses around them changed hands for ten and twenty times what they had paid. It had been redecorated periodically, but retained the style of the era when they moved in: austere and utilitarian, with white-walled, charcoal-grey and neutral-coloured rooms intended as a background for rational living. He had been attracted to Barbara because she seemed so rational. Nothing about their house reminded him of where he had lived until the age of twelve. The two interiors were entirely different.

Barbara had never shown any interest in how the house looked. As soon as the youngest of their three children started school she had trained and qualified as a social worker, and was out of the house all day and most evenings. Rudi, who had become an accountant after the war, found he was bringing more work home, and often spent whole days at his desk in the big open-plan all-purpose room on the ground floor.

There was nothing wrong with his corner – it had been especially planned so that everything necessary was within reach; but looking up from his desk one early winter afternoon he wondered at the many years spent in this bleak and characterless environment. At home, he thought – and became aware that home did not mean this house – everything had been so much prettier and more comfortable, more comforting, too; gratifying to the eye and the spirit in a way this room gave no indication of understanding or allowing for. He had a strong, momentary hallucination of his mother as she must have been in 1933 or '34, perfumed and elegantly dressed for the theatre, taking a few steps through the door and glancing around. He had become inured to and then unaware of the frayed, stained upholstery they had never bothered to replace after the children outgrew their destructive phase. Through her slightly slanted pale blue eyes he saw the muddy, formless paintings friends had given them years ago which remained the only decoration, and watched them narrow with distaste and incomprehension before she disappeared without having noticed him.

Walking home from the tube station next day, Rudi was surprised by the number of antique shops that had opened recently. A lamp on display was like one in the dining room of his childhood home. It had stood on the right-hand side of a large ornately carved sideboard, and he had loved those winter evenings when its opalescent glass shade glowed like a magic flower. Antique shops had always made him feel ignorant and gullible, but he forced himself to go inside. The lamp was more expensive than any comparable purchase and, writing a cheque, he sweated as heavily as if committing a shameful and dangerous act. Standing on his desk, the lamp's soft light made everything else in the room seem even more nondescript.

'That's new, isn't it?' Barbara remarked, tying a headscarf over her short blonde hair. 'I forgot my papers for a case conference, or I wouldn't have come back. I've left something in the oven for you and the children.'

'That's really beautiful. I'd like to do a drawing of it.' Faith was the elder of the two girls, and had just become an art student. Circumstances had made him an accountant, but Rudi often wondered if he had betrayed his potential. Faith was the only one of the children who took after him. It would be hard to guess that Mavis and Tony had a Jewish father. They favoured Barbara's side of the family.

Most men would be more likely to spend time at the weekend with a son rather than a daughter, but Tony had never given him an opportunity to develop that sort of relationship. When not at school the boy was out with friends: an eminently social being. Mavis, the baby, had been her mother's girl from the start, and so Rudi and Faith were left to make their own Saturday entertainment. Visiting museums and art galleries with her produced a combination of pleasure and anguish. He was grateful for an opportunity to revisit paintings and statues not seen for years. It was wonderful to watch Faith's knowledge and appreciation increase, to witness the development of this lovely, perceptive being. The anguish came when he remembered visiting museums with his mother and recognised the inherent quality of Faith's responses, so similar to hers; when he realised that his mother must have felt the same parental joy he did now.

Often they had set out with no particular destination or purpose, but now Rudi had an aim – the search for pictures, rugs, china, bits of furniture, anything that evoked his childhood home. Faith thought it perfectly natural to buy so much, and he found it easier to spend money in the company of his pretty, auburn-haired seventeen-year-old daughter than when alone. He had loved her from the first sight of her newborn face, with its unmistakable and strongly marked resemblance to his mother. The echoes and parallels and actual duplications between daughter and mother incremented like compound interest once he began to look for them. He vowed to do whatever possible to help her, as though the years torn from his mother's life could be made good if Faith were happy and fulfilled.

The difference in style between his recent acquisitions and the other furnishings gave the house a hybrid and disturbing appearance. Rudi was irritable and dissatisfied, suspecting he would never achieve a convincing reproduction of his parental home. It became harder to summon up his mother's image. The lamps and rugs and little tables were useless magic. Yet even the memory of that first, vivid return as the person she had been, rather than the dehumanised victim he imagined, was enough to change his relationship to everything.

Each day it was more difficult to believe that he and Barbara were actually husband and wife. She was so calm, so busy and mature – like a kindly, abstracted nurse. He'd had a nursemaid rather like Barbara when he was about six years old. Apart from commenting on the amount of money he must be spending, she was benignly indifferent to the transformation of the house. In bed, when the light was out and her warm, silent, acquiescent body lay nearby, he could not stop himself from thinking that she was his mother. But rather than inhibiting him, this image increased his sexual desires. Frequently, he felt about to burst into tears. The sight of his glaring eyes and pale, tense, puffy face in the bathroom mirror repelled him.

Rudi had avoided talking to the children about the war, the camps, or how he came to England and his parents died. He had never even attempted to explain their connection to Judaism. It was far too late now to begin, and he was bitterly ashamed of such cowardice. Of course his mother would have wanted her grandchildren to be told everything. Perhaps that was why she had come back and, because the action had not prompted fulfilment of his duty, the reason for her withdrawal. This thought put him into a deep depression for several days. The next Saturday afternoon, on the Portobello Road with Faith, he saw a dress very like one his mother used to wear, dangling from the rail of an old-clothes stall. It gave him an idea. If his mother would not appear of her own free will, dressing Faith in similar clothes might force a return.

Faith was delighted with the garment and hurried back to the empty house to try it on. When she came down the stairs Rudi was astounded by the resemblance. This was not a revenant or hallucination but a solid, breathing figure of flesh: his mother even before he had known her, before his birth, when she had been a young girl. Unaware that she was being used for conjuration, his daughter had innocently assumed the identity of the dead woman.

This was success beyond his imaginings. No doubt that his mother was in the room – but which and how many of her? There was the young girl incarnated by the natural laws of genetic inheritance in his once-more-recognisable daughter; the beloved being for whose appropriate setting every object had been purchased; and the one he never wanted to meet again, the victim who had haunted his adult life.

Perhaps the lamps and rugs were not meant to lure back the girl and untroubled woman, after all – but to ward off this one. Gaunt, dirty, cowed, huddled defensively near the foot of the staircase and wearing the threadbare clothes of a camp inmate, she glared with sick, unrecognising eyes. It made him want to die. He could see her and Faith at the same time, they were only a few feet apart, though inhabiting separate universes.

'Take off that dress,' he commanded. 'Go upstairs and take it off right now.'

'I don't want to take it off.' The concentration camp woman vanished at the sound of her voice. 'I love it. I want to wear it all the time.'

'You look stupid in that dress,' he said desperately. 'You look ridiculous.'

'I don't think I do.' Her expression was defiant and challenging.

The only way to control the fear of breakdown was to stiffen his spirit with anger. Faith could not understand what was happening. 'Take off that dress immediately or I'll tear it off.' Though he had never threatened violence before, she knew he would, yet she refused to obey and stood her ground.

It took less than a moment to cross the empty space between them. The cloth was soft and old and gave easily. She screamed with shock and fear. The turmoil of his emotions was sickening. He thought he would lose consciousness. She was in his power and he could not resist exercising that power; he was tormenting her as though she were his specially chosen victim. There must have been someone who singled out his mother in the same way.

She clutched the pieces of torn fabric across her small breasts and ran up the stairs shouting 'Fascist!', voice thick with tears. He opened the front door and walked out of the house.

It's dark and cold, but he walks rapidly ahead, with no plan or choice of direction, completely indifferent to where he is going, his mind empty. After a time, the emptiness on all sides makes him realise that he must have crossed the road on to Primrose Hill. He tries sitting down on a bench, but the moment he stops moving he is swamped by such self-contempt and self-loathing that he cannot bear it, and starts to walk again. He fears that if he goes back to the house he will break into Faith's room and beat her to death. His stride lengthens. He is walking down Park Road now, down Baker Street, crossing Piccadilly, crossing the river; a tall, thick-bodied man unable to stop walking. He is going to keep walking until a car knocks him down or someone fells him with a blow, until he reaches the end of his endurance and drops in his tracks.

MID-TERM

Caroline had already approached the front door several times that morning, hands stretched toward the large brass knob. It was September, still warm enough to go out dressed as she was, walk down the stairs and into the street. All she had to do was pick up her purse and keys and open the door.

Some days, alternatives hovered temptingly close, so that combing her hair, there seemed no reason not to continue the movement and score a pattern of bloody scratches down brow and cheeks nor, dialing her solicitor's telephone number, not to shout vile words into the mouthpiece rather than politely ask if she might speak to him. Signing her name at the end of a letter, the shape of the word sprouted thorns and hooks and drops of blood, and she snorted with bitter, half-fearful amusement to imagine how its recipient would respond if he were able to share that vision.

On such days she knew why being left-handed was regarded as sinister. Good joke. Such thoughts came as a relief. They couldn't be part of the plot. Everything went wrong on the left side: heart attack, colitis, varicose veins. Surely investigation would confirm that disease struck from the left, the devil's, side, that more left lungs were affected by consumption and cancer than right ones. Of course it must be so, for weren't the others *all right?* Pain was consciousness of the left. No wonder right-wingers could afford to be so metaphysical.

Her daughter had been crawling on all fours in the dream

last night – except that the child had not resembled her daughter, but was thinner, wild and neglected-looking, face glazed like that of a baby left out too long in the cold with nose unwiped. She seemed to be picking something up from the floor, wearing an old school dress so short it left her exposed. For a girl of her age, those buttocks seemed pathologically thin, even wasted. Instead of pubescent curves, the naked hindquarters of a wolf-child were revealed.

'You're not wearing any underwear!' Her tone was righteous and maternal.

The girl stared over one shoulder with glittering brown eyes, indifferent, dangerous. She was sure her daughter's blue eyes had never held such an expression. 'I've given up wearing underwear. We all have, at school.'

The way her head slewed heavily round reminded Caroline even in the dream of an object seen at her solicitor's office a few weeks before. It stood on the desk between them: a hollowed half-sphere lined with a reflecting mirror surface, inside which an orange plastic ball hung on a thin white elastic thread. They had both looked at it while talking, rather than at each other. Noting her interest, he had demonstrated how when the ball was touched it moved back and forth and round; how its reflection diminished and enlarged, approached, withdrew and circled the actual ball until the two became so confused that she felt them loop her like one of those devices of knotted rope and wooden balls used to hobble cattle on the pampas, and drag her inside its cold reverberating concavity. 'Nice little toy, isn't it?' he had said.

Caroline woke then – at least, she could remember nothing further. Imagine if we ran around exposed like dogs, she'd mused, trying to understand such a dream about her daughter. But the girl was away at school, her father in another country with another woman, and there was no one in the flat to help her forget it, or tease out its meaning. Instead, she had combed her hair, phoned the solicitor to settle the last details of the divorce, written what she hoped would be the final letter on the same subject to her husband, and managed to do these things quite calmly. Now she must see what would happen next to test her mastery over the ludicrous or threatening possibilities of everyday existence.

If she had a car, a stretch of motorway would be a good place to begin, but the car had gone when her husband did. A taxi would be too boxy. She wondered if the underground would seem crowded, whether a bus might be better. Walking through the park was impossible – she'd be far too easily spotted and followed. Probably a helicopter was the nearest to what she imagined at this moment as the ideal mode of travel, but hardly practical for her immediate purpose, which was to try to get out of the flat, to leave this place where she had been a self-made prisoner for the last eighteen days.

Most of the time it had rained, which softened the edges of the fact that she was incapable of passing through the front door. Doris, her cleaning woman, brought any letters and the bottle of milk upstairs, and after the third day, having examined the face of her employer and noted the emptiness of the refrigerator, volunteered to do some shopping. So she was not going to be starved out. She'd phoned to cancel appointments and had refused invitations, put off friends who'd suggested dropping in for a visit, and written to explain to others, expected on occasions still in the future, that those meetings were no longer possible. It took less than eighteen days to sever her links with whoever might have called themself either friend or acquaintance. Doris was the only person she'd seen. Doris could intervene and deal with whatever was necessary. She felt her life becoming simpler and purer; it was a relief to accept the obvious: other people were as uninterested in her as she was in any of them.

But although leaving the flat had become her paramount aim, a barrier more effective than the panelled wooden door blocked her passage through it. Outside, she would have no control. There would be so many more fissures for chaos to seep through and spread like the black mud of that Bihar earthquake she'd read about, when a man had been sucked down into a newly opened void, then ejected unhurt a few moments later in a gush of water and slime. She could not rely on such a rebirth.

Staring at her own reflection could sometimes calm her, as though that familiar combination of angles and textures and colours had the same concentrating power as an idol or a crystal ball to be the basis for a meditation on time and eternity. Though aware it was merely the intensification of an inexorable process, she noticed a new quality to her skin that morning. It was the first time the flesh had seemed so absolutely different to the dense, tight, mattly glowing substance she saw when looking at her daughter, or photographs of herself taken twenty years ago. What was really new, though, was her reaction. She remembered feeling the same excited joy when her periods started. Agatha began to menstruate last summer, and she had been disconcerted by her daughter's lack of excitement, as if the importance she had granted the experience was invalidated by this matter-of-fact acceptance. Instead of backache, headache, belly-ache – which was what she had complained of at the time – the girl said she felt fine and went out bicycling with a friend.

Head bent forward, Caroline stared at the smooth, paint-filled grain of the wooden door like a witch gathering all her own forces, and those of every spirit she could call on, for a spell strong enough to annihilate her most dangerous enemy. But the door neither vanished in a puff of smoke nor swung open on to the mass of struggling bodies and vehicles and noise she feared. Instead, drained by this futile attempt, she stepped backwards – which brought her into line with the hall mirror. If her expression were different, the woman could be called good-looking. She must have been in her late thirties or even a few years older. Dark blonde hair was combed back from a wide, bony forehead and held in place by a grubby white elasticated band. The nose was straight, the mouth not too thin nor too wide. The skin looked as though it had been tanned, then faded. There were heavy shadows under the dark blue eyes. She was broad-shouldered and wore a man's striped shirt. That was all she could see before the woman moved out of her line of vision.

Coming home one evening, Caroline's taxi had stopped for a red light at a railway bridge. A curved arc of metal struts topped a brick wall on which slogans were chalked and sprayed. A young man passed her window, moving rapidly backwards. She watched him diminish away over the hump of the bridge, arms waving and the white blur of his face fading into the darkness. It looked as though he were being pulled by a string attached between his shoulderblades, like a toy dragged by a giant child. That gesticulating figured implied he had been shouting, but there was no sound connected with the memory. When the traffic lights changed and the taxi moved forward he had disappeared. To see the woman retreat into and then move out of the mirror frame gave her a similar sensation of powerlessness.

Doris usually arrived at one o'clock. At the beginning, three or four years ago, it had seemed a good arrangement, because Caroline was rarely in the flat at that hour and Doris could work undisturbed. Then, the flat had also been inhabited by her husband, her daughter who was at day school, and an au pair girl. They were all busy and went out and came back into the flat frequently and without difficulty. But perhaps it had only been so easy to enter and leave for the very reason that other people were doing so. Caroline had taught geography for three days a week at the local comprehensive until the previous year. Her husband had lectured in the same subject at the university. He had a similar post now in the United States. As students of this discipline they met and married. It was ironic that, having been enthralled by the variety and size of the earth, its changes of climate and terrain, its mountains and river valleys, she was now restricted to this tiny territory, and could see no more of the world than was visible from her second-floor windows.

Walking from the large room at the front of the flat, through the hall and past her bedroom, along the corridor to the kitchen and the other rooms where the au pair used to sleep, Michael had his study and Agatha her bedroom, had become her only form of exercise. She paced the corridor scores of times a day. As she opened each door and glanced inside, there was so much to remember that she thought it could take years before she understood what had led to this moment.

A rattle of the letterbox might mean that Doris was coming in, delayed by a combination of events to be narrated over a cup of tea. Instead, she heard retreating footsteps and saw an envelope on the carpet.

'Dear Mrs White,' the writing on the single sheet of lined blue notepaper began. 'I want to let you know I won't be coming back to work for you any more, I just can't go on. I tried hard to help you, but it's too much for me, I tried to see your side but I always thought Mr White was very nice and felt sorry for him and your little girl. You are a very strange woman, it has been hard for me, I didn't want to leave you on your own but I can't take any more. Maybe it will be for the best or if I have done wrong I can't do otherwise. You are not at all like I thought at first. Yours truly, Doris Handle Handley.'

She did not know whether to scream, laugh, cry, or tear the sheet of paper into shreds. Before she could perform any of these actions, the knot of feelings seemed to diminish with the speed of a retreating space vehicle – or was it more like a sea urchin, or an unhusked chestnut? – something roughly spherical, of a grey-brown colour, with a matted spiny covering. She visualised it disappearing behind a low range of distant mountains against an eggshell-blue sky, in that smooth-finished sub-Dali style of science fiction illustration. When she looked down at Doris's letter again, it was like something found tucked away in the back of an old book, referring to events so long past that she was forced to smile remembering how they had moved her.

After a while she went to make some tea. The half empty bottle of milk she took out of the refrigerator was the last. There were tins and packets in the cupboard, but not much fresh food. She would have to decide what to do now that Doris would no longer serve as her contact with the outside world.

It was possible to phone shops and arrange to have supplies delivered; to call the porter and ask him to bring the milk and post upstairs. But all this (apart from the letters which could enter the flat without her cooperation) would involve people ringing the bell and even perhaps expecting to come inside; would mean, more than anything, having to open the door. It had been all right until now, because Doris had a key and could let herself in with no disturbance. But the key was in the bottom of the envelope containing that letter, so there was no doubt that her decision was final. Doris's defection might be considered as a message to sit tight: that her attempt to go out, earlier that day, had been totally misguided. Otherwise, this letter would not have arrived so promptly. Until now her behaviour might have been labelled self-indulgent. But if she was to be deprived of the necessities of life, every action took on a more serious aspect, and she became more committed to its implications.

The last time Caroline left the flat was to take her daughter to the school train. The platform had been crowded with tanned, uniformed girls and their families. Most of them seemed genuinely pleased to exchange a strained, demanding home atmosphere, where they were never sure exactly what to say or do nor what the current attitude towards them might be, for the limited security of communal life. It was the start of her third year, and Agatha was used to it now. Caroline wondered if it had not been the parching emotional climate at home, rather than the effects of school, which had changed her so decisively.

It was not that she and Michael sat down to decide what to do. They had both been far too desperate and unhappy for anything so reasonable. The bewildered eleven-year-old flinched from her mother's nervous rages, and Michael's behaviour implied that he had organised Agatha's departure as a protective measure. Caroline felt even worse when she realised that she was the threat from which her daughter had to be rescued.

When Michael came home one day and, with no other clue than a gleeful smile, led Caroline to the front window and pointed down to the road outside, she could not understand what he was trying to convey. Finally, unnerved by the failure of his dumb show, he was forced to explain that he had traded in their navy blue family saloon for the glistening purple sports car at the kerbside. At that moment she knew he would soon leave her. During the next school holiday Agatha brought a lanky Australian friend to stay. The two girls were thrilled to go for drives whenever Michael needed to imagine how very like a glossy magazine advertisement they must look to whoever noticed them speeding towards the North Circular.

Between Easter and the summer holiday, the decision to separate was finalised. Caroline went to a friend's villa in Spain while Michael took Agatha for a long camping trip. She arrived home to find them already back. Agatha knew now that he was leaving. Her eyes were guarded and critical when she looked at Caroline, yearning when turned towards her father, but she said nothing, and in the days between Michael's departure for America and Agatha's return to school, Caroline had not found a way to break through the distrustful formality of her daughter's defences. Though it was less than a month since Agatha had gone back to school, she would have been dreading the next holiday already if it were possible to believe that life would continue along foreseeable lines.

After a day of sunshine the sky was intensifying into neon-mauve. Caroline stood at the window looking down at the cars moving slowly northwards, bumper to bumper at times until the hold-up cleared and the stream would thin and disperse. The excitement of dusk left her unmoved. It was later, when the cars had been put away in their garages or stood outside on the street and their drivers were eating or watching television, when theatres and cinemas were crowded with the last-show audiences, and dinner-party guests, overfed, moved away from the table, that she began to suffer. Again she heard Michael's accusations and Agatha's evasive dismissals. The words of Doris's letter returned as if she were reading it for the first time. The three of them were present in the unlit room, stepping out from and then back into the confusing shadows; their separate statements combining, like an operatic trio, into a unified assault.

Too frightened to turn away even for a moment, she dragged her feet backwards over the thick pile carpet until the hard security of the wall pressed against her shoulderblades, then slid down to huddle with knees drawn up to her chin and arms locked protectively around them. The beams of passing head-lamps marched from one wall to the other and splayed across the ceiling, revolved over her face, and drained away into the darkest corner under the far window. A hand slid beneath her bare thigh and the fingers brushed against the fullness between her legs and pushed aside the cloth. It took only a few minutes to reach orgasm, and when she had recovered, those threatening presences were gone.

The flat soon looked neglected, but that was only part of the difference. Expecting Doris, she had felt obliged to present an appearance of normality. Now, she did not trouble to get out of pyjamas and dressing gown. Though she had smoked ten to fifteen cigarettes a day all her adult life and had thought she was dependent on coffee, she did not seem to miss either when supplies ran out. The drinks cupboard was bare, but alcohol had never been important.

From the first day, it had been impossible to switch on the radio or television set. Whenever she tried, the hand extended towards the appropriate knob froze, as if it knew better than she did that each apparatus was an open channel of influence and attack. One afternoon, feeling an imperative need to hear another voice, Caroline dialled the speaking clock. The bland female tones droned on, dividing the flow of time into tiny segments until she dropped the phone on to the floor.

Clashing dustbin-lids announced the start of each new day. She would turn restlessly in the crumpled bed that had not been made or changed since Doris's departure, pull sheet and blankets around her ears, and drift back into a state of half-sleep she tried to make last as long as possible. Eventually, she would have to get up. Through those windows opening on to the inner courtyard, bursts of sound forced an awareness of other people's lives, or a too-loud radio provided unwanted information. The central heating had clanked into life, which meant that October the first must have passed. When she wanted to eat or drink she went down the corridor to the kitchen. Emptied cereal packets, torn biscuit wrappings and opened tins lay where they had fallen. The next meal would have to be a choice between a tin of unsweetened chestnut purée or one of okra. A few evenings ago, she had boiled the last of the rice in the only clean pot. There was still some left, but it had gone sour.

The days were shortening. When dusk came, Caroline moved through the flat putting on every light. Sometimes she remembered to switch them off, but other nights they went on burning until the following evening, when she would be pleased to find the room already illuminated. Then she forgot about them, and apart from those that had burned out, and the bedroom, which she still darkened after crawling into bed, all lamps remained permanently lit.

A whole afternoon could pass while she lay on the bed or floor. As far as she knew, her mind was empty. Then she began to dream about Agatha again. This girl raged and shouted abuse, threw whatever was nearest to hand, slammed doors, and refused to listen when Caroline attempted to say something – none of which had ever happened; though Caroline

94

remembered how badly she had behaved at the same age. She had been grateful for Agatha's equanimity, sensing that should her daughter show the same uncontrolled temper, she would not be able to deal with it. At times she suspected that Agatha held back in order to spare her. But she had also felt a disappointed hostility, as though her own irritability was the sign of a superior nature. The dreams provided the zest and excitement of battle, and an intimate contact which had not been possible since Agatha's childhood.

In spite of increasing weakness, she tried to keep clean, though the effort of a bath now daunted her. One morning it seemed too much trouble to get out of bed. She didn't feel hungry any more. She wasn't even thirsty. But although the outline of objects was blurred, colours were more intense. The fluting of the curtains' folds and the changing shades of their stripes as the light altered, the weave and gloss of the shiny bedspread, the glitter and shadow of bottles on the dressing table, were totally satisfying. Surely this was the peace of mind she had sought so long. When the front door of the flat opened Caroline was too absorbed to hear it, and would have been too feeble to turn her head if she had.

'I haven't seen your mother for weeks, my dear,' the porter said as he took his master key out of the lock, half-turning to the young girl in a grey school coat who followed close at his heels. 'Are you sure she knew you were coming home?'

'I didn't get a letter to say she wouldn't be here,' Agatha answered defensively, trying to look over his shoulder. She was blonde like her mother, and almost as tall.

'I tell you what,' he continued, as they entered the hall where lights glowed inappropriate for the time of day. 'You sit here and I'll go and make sure everything's all right.'

Agatha was uneasy enough to be glad to obey any firm adult command, even one from the porter.

When he saw the debris of Caroline's last meals, he whistled thoughtfully, passed one hand over his sallow, half-bald head, and closed the kitchen door. 'I should have come up sooner,' he muttered to himself. 'Well, there's no one down this end,' he called in a cheerful voice, too loud now that he was back in the hall. 'She must have gone off somewhere and forgot to let you know.' The girl looked even more forlorn and he felt sorry for her. 'I'll just check the sitting-room, to make sure she's not having a nap or something. Now you stay here, don't you move, all right?' He suspected that Mrs White might have done something silly. He was a grown man who'd been through the war, in some pretty nasty spots, and he'd seen odd things here in the flats as well, and he had the feeling that this was no place for a young girl.

Agatha noticed that her mother's bedroom door was open. Only the foot of the bed was visible, but she was sure that someone lay in it. She remembered it looking exactly like that when she'd been little, and had run into the room to climb in beside Caroline. She squinted and leaned forward, tethered by the last threads of her own reluctance and obedience; then she rushed across the hall and through the bedroom door.

'My God, how awful!' she screamed. The porter was there in a moment. It was like a concentration camp photo – one of those old women from some famine or war – all the horror pictures she hadn't been able to avoid or forget, whose living models she'd hoped never to have to see.

'I'm sure she's alive,' the porter said. Her wrist was warm and he could feel a pulsing there. He put an arm around Agatha's shoulders. 'You can't do anything for her now. Have a good cry if you feel like it, and I'll phone the hospital.'

Agatha shrugged his arm away. Her cheeks were as wet as though a jug of water had been thrown in her face. She knelt by the side of the bed holding Caroline's hand and looking at her as if only by the intensity and concentration of that gaze would her mother be held back from slipping over the edge of life. The porter stayed with them until the ambulance came, then went down to the basement to get his wife, so they could clear up the worst of the mess.

HOUSES

They had been in the house for six years, since coming back to England when James retired. Their married son and daughter lived some distance from the seaside town, and most of the time the tall rooms prepared for family visits stood empty.

Being so large, the house made a lot of work. A charwoman came in three mornings a week, but after forty years as the wife of a government official, able to keep her home exactly as she wished with the help of several servants, Yvonne Fletcher's standards were high. She was not aware that her demands were unusual or excessive, nor that altered circumstances might modify them. A house must look a certain way. Each object must be cleaned, polished, smoothed – whatever treatment was necessary to cherish and conserve it.

Some of the furniture and ornaments were from her side of the family, others from James's. Apart from an abstract respect for craftsman and ancestor, decades of living with these objects had transformed them into tangible records of her taste and choice, materialised memories as symbolic as altar decorations. While James pottered with his books and papers, worked in the garden or took slow walks along the seafront, Yvonne would dust and polish the special pieces, then sit in her pale green silk-covered armchair knitting squares which would later be sewn into bedspreads for her children, or some charitable purpose.

She was a thin, pretty woman of sixty-four, with short, waved grey hair, pale grey eyes, and a well-powdered sallow face. She dressed carefully and wore rubber or cotton gloves for housework, so when she finished and put her rings back on – engagement ring and wedding band and the small sapphire from her grandmother – she still had the appearance of a leisured lady expecting an afternoon visit. Her nature was gentle and optimistic, as if nothing had happened to destroy her belief that some secret, appropriate order existed even though she might never be able to understand it.

When certain pains became too persistent to ignore Yvonne went to a doctor, then to a specialist, then into hospital for tests. It was an unpleasant process. She remembered reading of ivory figurines which Chinese women had used to indicate their pain's location: one for those in chest or upper regions, another for below the waist. The second would have served her. The radium treatment made her ill, she ached everywhere and became thinner. Each fortnight when the ambulance brought her home, James seemed more absorbed and silent, more perturbed. The ambulance men would help her into bed, then go away. James made lemon tea, for the idea of anything else to eat or drink nauseated her. He had been handsome – but now Yvonne saw an old man with white hair and faded eyes, skin stained by years of sun. He was stooped, not tall any longer; as if since coming back to England he had not wanted to look anyone in the face.

Their friends were from the old days. Visits were exchanged less frequently than letters, and it was she who wrote them. It was only now, when she could do nothing to help, that she realised how well he had concealed the lack of anything to interest or occupy him. The pleasure with which he brought tea, smoothed her pillow, sat by her bedside or went to the kitchen to prepare a meal, revealed how useless he had felt.

As soon as she could, Yvonne would resume the normal activities of mistress of the house. But she was weak. It was impossible to deny that she could not manage. For the first time in their married life she asked his advice about domestic matters, broke through the barrier which had compartmentalised their areas of responsibility. It was strange to be discussing these problems with him rather than a woman friend, almost heady. In spite of the pain and weakness which made her feel so deathly-old, such conversation was like a return of youth, of their very first days together, before she had realised he was too busy, that it was not suitable to trouble one's husband this way. Perhaps because she was seven years younger, his preoccupations had always seemed more important.

James insisted he would take care of the arrangements, and next morning set out for the Labour Exchange. He must have hired hundreds of men in his time, but had never before tried to find a woman for the house. He returned home, relieved to be in its familiar chilly silence again, baffled and diminished by the petty officiousness of the place he had visited, and the reminder of his present superfluous condition. He changed into the pair of old dancing slippers he was wearing out around the house. Yvonne lay on her side. She had fallen asleep while he was away. Her face was more flushed than usual and she looked younger, yet there was something tense in her posture, as if even now she were suffering. He left the bedroom and went into his own next door, sat down squarely in his armchair and stared across to the opposite wall where a map of Africa hung, waiting until she awoke.

Yvonne was sitting in her green chair when the young woman arrived. It was one of her good days. James left them alone and waited until he heard the front door close before going downstairs.

'She seemed pleasant,' Yvonne said. 'Perhaps a little strange. Not the sort of person I would have expected to apply for the job. Her name is Rachel Scott. She's separated from her husband, and living with her parents. She said she's a writer, that's why she wants a part-time job.' They looked at each other with shared suspicion of anyone who would label herself so. 'But I think she'll be all right,' Yvonne smiled reassuringly. 'After all, no one else has come. She looked sensible enough. I'm tired now, my dear. I think I'll go and lie down.'

Rachel arrived at nine o'clock the next morning. She would come every day at that time, six days a week; tidy, dust and make beds, supervise the charwoman and cook lunch for herself and the Fletchers. After clearing up the meal she would leave. Yvonne was between two treatments and therefore able to explain the routine. By the second morning she could see that the young woman was competent to manage everything in the house.

Rachel Scott was a plain, dark girl of twenty-three. Her determination to get away from home had led to an unsuitable marriage to a salesman who travelled for most of each week, and though she found an office job in the Midland town where he was based, she was bored and lonely. At an evening class she met a local writer who soon seduced her and, which she came to regard as more important, persuaded her to start writing. When her husband learned about this affair he neglected to return from one of his selling trips, sending instead a letter informing Rachel that he had taken up residence in another town with a lady whom he deeply loved. After several weeks alone in the room she had shared with him, Rachel realised that his departure had improved nothing. Her job was dull and so was the local writer. She took a train south and settled back into her old room at home. Her determination to be a writer made it easy to ignore her mother's questions about future plans, and her father's hints that he was not prepared to support her indefinitely. It was determination which gave a fixed and stubborn look to her narrow, closely set brown eyes. When she found this part-time housekeeping job, it seemed an ideal solution.

Strange to leave her parents' house each morning for another with an even more oppressive atmosphere, to journey back one generation further. Both her mother's and father's parents had been dead since she could remember. Perhaps through contact with the Fletchers she would discover more about her own family. Rachel's father was the manager of a hardware shop. Her grandfathers had both been small tradesmen. In spite of the difference in social and economic status, the fact that Yvonne and James were approximately the same age her grandparents would have been, had lived through the same historical events and been formed by the same general ideas, convinced her that similarities were more significant than any differences. Through this job she was licensed to study the Fletchers, to speculate about the meaning of what they did and had done. She was fascinated by them, and curiosity justified monotony, among other things.

Yvonne watched Rachel dust the mementoes displayed on fragile tables, the top of the piano, and along the mantelshelf. At that moment, she was passing the yellow cloth across a photograph of Yvonne's grandchildren, and remarked, 'What nice-looking kids.'

'Yes, they are,' Yvonne agreed. 'Do you like children?'

'I don't really know. I've never had much to do with them.'

'Wouldn't you like to have some of your own one day?'

Rachel hesitated. 'I imagine they must tie you down awfully. How can you ever be free once you have a child?'

Yvonne smiled uneasily. Freedom was an abstraction she had never been able to relate to her own life. Warming to the subject, Rachel continued, 'You might stay with your husband just for that reason. Suppose you wanted to leave him, or discovered he was having an affair, but didn't want to take the child away from its father?'

'How idealistic you sound,' Yvonne murmured. She had forgotten there were other pains than physical ones. It was so long since that place had been probed; she'd thought it healed or scarred to insensibility. 'That is why children are a blessing. What foolish and damaging things would be done if they did not keep the true values before one's eyes.'

'I can't imagine trusting anyone enough to have a child,' Rachel muttered, half to herself, putting the silver-framed photograph back on to the piano.

'My daughter-in-law once came to me, when the older child was still a baby. She was almost crying, she said Bobby was seeing some other woman and she didn't know what to do. But I told her to take her joy from the child. Then she had another, and now they're such a happy family, and we've never mentioned that talk again.' She felt better, thinking about her daughter-in-law and her problems. The advice she gave, the only thing she knew to say – traditional advice which had sustained her at one time – was as successful as ever; such mixed success being all life ever allowed. What could not be labelled absolute failure was regarded as success: this was the law of reality as she had learned it.

A system that countenanced such wisdom, such truths, had nothing to do with her, Rachel thought angrily. She would never submit to its control. But in the tone of Yvonne's voice (though she did not understand its significance) she recognised the muffled grief of millions of frightened women. Sadness and anger concealed her own fear. When she turned around, Yvonne had slumped down into the chair.

It was raining next morning. Autumn was coming early. Inside the house light lay on all polished surfaces like congealed mutton fat. As Rachel arrived, James walked through the back door with a filled coal scuttle. 'I'm going to make a fire for Yvonne.' He passed a hand over his head, then wiped a film of moisture from the shoulders of his tweed jacket.

'I can do it,' Rachel offered.

'I like making fires. Not that I made many until we came back home.' Yvonne had begun to tell Rachel about their life in Africa, but James rarely talked to her. She wondered what he did in his room.

'Shall I clean your room for you?' The two elderly people

barely disturbed the house. Dust settled rather through absence of movement.

'Thank you.' He picked up the scuttle again and went into the lounge.

His room was extraordinarily neat; high narrow bed made with military exactitude, no clothing in sight, papers on the desk arranged in piles which lay at right angles to its corners. It looked bleak and sad, like the room of a lonely schoolboy. She examined a row of books along the mantelshelf: military memoirs, practical mathematics, Kipling. Above the fireplace hung a photo of a group of young men, one of whom must have been James Fletcher, and behind the brushes on the bureau stood a sepia portrait-study of Yvonne taken when she was a young woman, a child at each side – the archetypal family picture one would expect to find in some far outpost of Empire, in just the sort of Spartan surroundings which James had managed to recreate in a first-floor English seaside bedroom.

She bent to examine his papers while cursorily dragging the dustcloth around the desk. Some were bills, there was a letter she assumed to be from his son by the few lines that caught her eye concerning the iniquitous rise in the children's school fees, and a pile of typewritten sheets of paper standing next to some faded exercise books. She opened the door softly and listened. The house was as quiet as before. Yvonne must still be asleep from her tablets, and he still busy with the fire. She went back to the desk and lifted the blank top sheet of paper covering what was written – which seemed to be an account of his years of professional service: interesting enough, but not the revelation she had hoped for. Disappointed, and slightly ashamed of herself, she put the papers back in place and quickly finished the room.

'Is that you, Rachel?' Yvonne called. She sat by the bed in a wooden-armed chair, dressed in an old plaid dressing gown. Her hair was untidy and her face very pale. 'Would you please make me some tea?' The room was furnished with the marital bedroom suite: brought back to England with them, and probably shipped out from England in the first place – worn now, pretty and no longer in fashion; the large wardrobe and curved dressing table inlaid with contrasting woods, the chests, bedside tables and bed she must have chosen so carefully as a bride.

'How do you feel this morning?' It pained Rachel to see her looking so ill. 'Much the same,' Yvonne admitted.

'Have a cup with me,' she invited as Rachel returned. 'There shouldn't be too much to do this morning.' Apart from the unmade bed her room was scrupulously tidy. 'I can't remember what I used to do – but I seemed to keep busy. Now I wonder why I never found time for anything else. When you're well, you think you'll live forever, and don't realise that time has value. And you think it doesn't make any difference how you die. You know you'll die one day, but when you hear about someone dying slowly and painfully, you just think – oh well, that's how it happens. I've learned it's not like that at all. There is a difference between a painful death and a peaceful death – because until you do die, you are alive. It's still a part of your life, not of your death.' Rachel was so unlike any person she knew or could remember, it seemed possible to speak aloud what otherwise would have to remain unsaid.

'I wish we could forget about dying,' Rachel said gloomily.

'When I was your age,' Yvonne reminisced, 'an old aunt of mine was dying. I saw her quite often – my mother took me there. They were sisters, and very close. My aunt lay in bed, her husband was dead already and she'd never had any children, so she was alone in her house except for a couple of servants. To me she seemed already dead – but in spite of all her pain she wanted to go on living, to stretch her time out as far as she could.' Rachel wondered if she felt the same; but sensed the question would lower Yvonne's opinion of her.

A few days later Yvonne asked her to open the wardrobe and bring certain garments over to the bed. 'I know that neither my daughter nor daughter-in-law would like these dresses,' she explained. 'Aren't they lovely?' There was an afternoon frock from the thirties, fine bias-cut gauze printed with blurred yet childish flowers in green and orange, its skirt and sleeves wide flounces of cloth. 'They'd only laugh at them and throw them away, and I think they'd suit you beautifully.'

'How did you know I'd love clothes like these?' Rachel said appreciatively, stroking the pleated bodice of a peach-coloured crepe dress.

'I guessed,' Yvonne laughed. Her face was the colour of putty, gums and whites of eyes stained the same earthy hue. 'I'm going to the hospital this afternoon for another treatment, so I wanted to show them to you. Would you like to take them home? Take that blue one as well. It should fit you. I used to have a good figure, you know.' She smiled coquettishly, then the expression changed to a grimace of pain. 'Would you ask James to come up for a moment?' Her voice was plaintive, in spite of her effort to control it.

Lunch was even more silent than usual. The dining room was never used for this meal, and James and Rachel sat at the small wooden kitchen table. The tiled floor, polished the day before, glowed a virulent red, and the brass doorknob bright against the dark green pantry door hypnotically attracted her gaze.

'Would you like me to make some soup before I go, for you to heat up tonight?' she asked, trying to begin a conversation with the sad old man who stared over her left shoulder at the wall opposite.

'Don't trouble yourself, my dear,' he murmured.

She was touched by this address. 'But I'd like to.'

'You told my wife that you were a writer.' He shifted his eyes away from the cream blankness and refocused on her face. 'Do you write every day after you leave here?'

'I try to,' Rachel answered, excited yet disconcerted by his interest. 'If the weather is good I usually walk along the seafront and think about what I did the day before, and how to carry on. Then I go home and try to get it down on paper.'

'What do you write about?' He was interested, she was sure.

'I'm working on a novel. I suppose it's about my life.'

This personal revelation deflected his curiosity, as if he found the subject somehow unseemly. 'I suppose one's own life is the best material,' he conceded after a pause. 'It sounds a very lonely existence. Do you see any friends?'

'Not really,' she admitted defensively. 'I used to know people here, before I got married, but now we don't seem to have much in common. Anyway, I prefer to use my time to think and try to understand my life, rather than meaningless chatter.'

'You sound like someone older, if you'll forgive me making a personal comment.'

'Of course,' she answered, flushing. She regarded it as a compliment. 'Have you ever written anything?' She had a clear vision of the pile of papers on his desk.

'I've been looking through some old notebooks I kept when I was a young man. But the idea of someone my age trying to write must seem comic to you.'

'Not at all,' she assured him. 'I imagine your notebooks are fascinating.'

He glanced at her mistrustfully. 'I doubt if you'd find them interesting,' he mumbled.

Confused by this change of mood, Rachel did not know how to break the silence again. A short time later, the ambulance arrived. She and Yvonne left the house together. It was raining heavily. One of the men held an umbrella over Yvonne's head as he helped her down the path. Rachel went to the bus stop. There would be no walk along the seafront today.

Two stories sent to magazines were waiting when she arrived home. They had been returned with a printed rejection slip only, not a word to explain why or suggest she send other work. Her parents were out and she was glad of that, too discouraged to tolerate or ward off questions. Her room looked squalid in the grey afternoon light – bed unmade, clothes scattered about, papers in disorder on the small table. The reason for her present way of life evaded her. All she knew was that she was as bored and lonely as ever. Yvonne's imminent death oppressed her with a helpless irritation, a need to assert her own youth and health. She wanted to be courted and desired, or even better, to be in love. Instead, she went to her desk and began to write a new story.

James sat at the kitchen table with a cup of stale tea in front of him, looking as if he had been there for a very long time. Rachel asked about Yvonne.

'She's still asleep. She has so little relief that when she can forget her pain for a moment I'm grateful.'

'I'll be very quiet.' She took her coat off and began to carry plates from the table to the sink.

'I don't want to go upstairs in case I wake her,' he explained. 'I hope I'm not in your way.'

'I'll do some ironing, then I won't disturb her, either. Everything I need is in the cupboard here.' She set up the board and spread a shirt over it.

'Now you've come I think I'll go out for some fresh air.' He pushed himself away from the table and walked stiffly out of the room.

About an hour later Rachel heard something, and went into the hall. It was like the eerie gabbling of a flight of witches overhead, a hollow unlocatable echo reminding her that James had not yet returned, that she was alone with these noises which surely could only be made by someone in extremity. For one moment she wanted to run away, abandon the house and the dying woman whom she could picture half-fallen from the bed, clawing at her body in agony, babbling her hoarse despair. Then she nerved herself to do whatever was necessary.

The door of Yvonne's room stood a few inches ajar. All she could see through this narrow slit, when it became visible as she reluctantly climbed the stairs, was pale morning light on the faded carpet. Without knocking, she pushed the door back. It took a few seconds to absorb the peaceful scene of Yvonne sitting up in bed with the telephone in her hand.

She smiled distractedly, nodding a greeting above the receiver. Rachel slumped against the door frame. Some acoustical freak had magnified Yvonne's voice and sent it echoing through the house.

'I was talking to my daughter,' Yvonne explained. 'I shall be going into hospital, and it would be nice if she could visit me at home before I leave. I think hospital visits are rather disturbing for children, don't you?'

'When will you be going?'

'Oh, quite soon.'

'But how long will you be there?' Rachel pressed. She did not want Yvonne to go away, did not want anything to change. Whatever happened, she would be responsible now; had released, by her vivid imaginings, a potential which otherwise might not have been able to exist.

'My dear child, how can I say?' Yvonne recognised that she might have been touched by the girl's concern if it were not that her pain was increasing each moment. 'Will you bring some tea?' she asked, wanting to be alone and swallow another tablet as soon as possible.

James was sitting in the same pose Rachel had found him earlier. When the tea was ready he said he would take it upstairs. The mood in the house was now one of acknowledged crisis. There seemed no point in trying to follow the daily routine. The kitchen had lost its reassuring air. She could easily imagine how it would appear to the next occupiers, stripped of the Fletchers' possessions, before they disguised its bareness with their own.

'When will Yvonne go into hospital?' she asked.

'Ah, so she told you. I was about to.'

'What are you going to do?'

'We're having Yvonne transferred to a hospital near my son's home,' James said. 'I shall stay there. It seems the best way. That hospital is better than the local one, I understand.' He sat on the opposite side of the table, chair turned at an angle so that he could look into the hall rather than at her face. His voice was low but matter-of-fact, his features even more expression-less than usual. Because of her own agitation, she longed to see some sign of emotion from him.

'Is there anything I can do for her now?' Rachel asked.

'I don't think so.'

She was afraid she might burst into tears. 'Shall I cook lunch for you? There must be something I could do.'

'You've been very helpful to us while you've been here, Rachel.' He looked directly at her now, and spoke as clearly as if to a child or a foreigner or one of his African assistants. 'I shall always be grateful to you. I don't want to eat anything for the moment. Perhaps it would be best if you just tidied up and then went home. Tomorrow we can talk about what will happen – '

'Shall I take Yvonne another cup of tea?'

'I think she'd prefer to be alone now,' he stated firmly.

In a few minutes she was walking towards the seafront. A strong wind blew and the waves were high, almost brown except where a diffused glare from the flat grey sky brought out a muddy turquoise colour. The few other people she saw were far apart, spaced out across the promenade, as if no one wanted to be close to anyone else. Rachel pulled her coat collar up. She could not face the thought of going back to her parents' empty house for the rest of the day. She kept walking until she reached the central section of the seafront, passing closed stalls and cafés and chained, plastic-sheeted piles of folded deckchairs. An amusement arcade was still open, a jukebox echoing hollowly from its almost unpeopled interior. She hadn't entered it for years, not since she'd been part of a group of schoolgirls with linked arms, laughing and pushing each other as they hurried to experience its delights. She felt in her pocket for some loose change. She would stand by a machine and start to play, and soon, she knew, one of the men or boys would come over and talk to her.

JUNE AND NELLY

Rain saturated the spongy fields, the flocks of sheep with fleece the yellow-grey of filthy linen, their bleating silenced by persistent drizzle. A smell like boiling cabbage exhaled from the wet greenness of blossoming orchards and white nettle flowers edging the ditch. A couple were walking down the road's puddled macadam. She held an umbrella over their heads, he held her arm. The awkwardness of their linked progress made it seem as though she were leading him.

The man gazed above the hedge-tops into the uniform grey of the low sky with a dreamy, boyish expression, but there were lines around the blue eyes under the peak of his cap. The woman wore a vivid silk headscarf. Her features were heightened by mascara, eyeshadow and lipstick, as if that morning, like every other, she had felt the need to assert her own existence against the indifferent expanse of fields beyond the bedroom window.

The road curved, and set back from the bend was a shabby farmhouse, with cowsheds and a large concreted yard. An old man opened to their knock. His smile was barely friendly, but he exchanged their empty eggboxes for full ones willingly enough. No one had managed to discover much about the newcomers. He did not visit the pub, she rarely shopped in the general store, and they had not put in an appearance at church. The household included no children as sources of information. The only material evidence the village had to ponder was the unfamiliar sight of a house blazing lights from ground floor to attic long after others had been darkened.

The front of the house was overshadowed by trees, but the kitchen faced west and, even when the sun was not shining, by late afternoon was the most pleasant room to be in, the large dresser stacked with blue and white china and the Aga warm and domestic. Paul hung up his coat and cap then put the kettle on. Nelly removed her mackintosh and boots more slowly and climbed the stairs to the bedroom. It was hands that gave your age away, she thought, seated at the dressing table, studying her new wedding band and the old one, the diamond and sapphire engagement ring from her first husband and the opal and pearl one that had been her father's eighteenth-birthday present, the cornelian seal ring passed down from mother to daughter and the yellow topaz Paul gave her on their honeymoon. In spite of creams, nail-polish and these ornaments, her well-kept hands showed the veins and marks and tendons of a middle-aged woman, and damp weather made the joints ache.

'Tea's ready, dear. I'll take it into my study.' She heard the cups rattle in their saucers as he crossed the hall. The large fire-place, and walls already lined with bookshelves, had been one of the deciding factors in the choice of this particular house. It was to create the ideal conditions for his writing that she had bought it. How noble and proud he is, she thought, enchanted by his quick movements – it's that adolescent quality of a poet. 'Nelly, darling.' He bent over the chair to embrace her. 'Everything's so wonderful. I can hardly believe my luck.'

Nelly Delmont (as she was then) had come to England the previous winter especially to meet Paul Newingbury, her daughter's fiancé. For most of her life she had moved between Europe and America – wherever circumstance led or there were friends and family. She had always been rich, and her first husband worked for a multinational company, so she was used to changing homes every year or two. His death in a car crash altered that pattern for a while, but when June, their only child, went off to boarding-school, old habits reasserted themselves.

'I'll leave you to get on with your work,' she said when tea was finished. Paul agreed, too preoccupied with the problem of what to do with himself to wonder how Nelly passed these hours. He was not yet accustomed to such lavishness of space and time. On the new, gleaming leather surface of the desk his ink-stained folders looked poor and shabby, disturbingly slender.

The past few months had transformed his existence. Instead of being a bachelor of thirty living in a bed-sitting-room in Tufnell Park, he was settled in a splendid country house with this marvellous woman. The fact that she was fourteen years older only increased a mysteriousness which nothing in his background helped him to understand. While he had grown up in straitened decency over his parents' newsagent's shop and managed by sheer hard work to get to university and become a teacher, Nelly was flying around the world, part of a cosmopolitan, multi-lingual tribe; already a married woman when he was a schoolboy, a widow by the time he became a man, a mother before he knew the facts of life.

June had seemed enough of an exotic to him, when they met at a friend's party almost two years before, already beyond his expectations or entitlement. But: 'You *are* a greedy boy!', they'd always said at home, even in his infant days. He wanted everything, and it never made any difference that the desired object might already belong to someone else or that there were other reasons why he should not have it. Through the reaction of parents, teachers, classmates and neighbours he learned the need to hide such cravings, but they never diminished. When he saw Nelly he knew that by comparison to what had satisfied him until now, she was the grandest prize of all.

He remembered going with June to Heathrow. The plane from New York was late, and they were jaded and irritable when Nelly finally emerged from Customs. He had imagined a haggard, ageing sophisticate, not this vivid being swathed in dark furs, eyes glittering with excitement as she hugged June and

113

began to press gifts on to them, meanwhile pouring out a stream of news about cousins and friends and what she had been doing which left his head in a whirl. Afterwards, he was sure it had been love at first sight.

'Ridiculous and horrible. How else would you describe it? Your mother must be a monster.' The speaker of these words was almost trembling with fervour. Electric light outlined short curls of fair hair and an aquiline curve of nose and brow as she bent urgently forward towards June, slumped in the shabby armchair opposite.

'Leave me alone, Margaret. I don't want to think about it.'

'Maybe you don't, but I can't think about anything else. I still can't believe it's true. I've never heard anything like it. As for Paul – I never trusted him. I told you he was no good, didn't I?' Margaret had seen her mother so badly treated by husband and sons that she had vowed at an early age never to have anything to do with a man. She qualified as a librarian, and gradually rose to senior position in a branch library. When June applied for a job there, she liked the look of the younger woman and accepted her although she was less qualified than the other candidates. 'Poor darling,' she went on, reaching for the whisky bottle on the floor by her chair. 'Let me give you another one.'

'We've been getting drunk every night for weeks,' June remarked petulantly, holding out her glass to be filled. It was strange how much she resembled her mother. Yet the soft features, straight brown hair and large dark eyes which made Nelly so intriguingly attractive, in June's case had a blurred, pugnacious quality, though she shared Nelly's trait of seeming younger than her age of twenty-five. All through childhood this similarity was commented upon – which had been emphasised by the fact that Nelly made sure their outfits were always the same colour. June would never forget that moment when, instead of feeling proud and delighted to hear once again that

114

remark, 'Why, the two of you could be sisters!', rage and embarrassment had transfixed her. She had stayed in England after finishing school, and taken any job available in order to prove that she could manage perfectly well on her own.

'Well, it's better than going to bed to cry,' Margaret said, pouring another drink for herself. 'You were in a sorry state when I found you.' And indeed, if Margaret had not been prompted to visit her, June thought she might well have lain in bed until dead of misery and indifference.

When her friend's consoling embraces altered in character, the intensity of her own response was a cause of confusion and alarm. But at least it stopped her thinking about what Paul and Nelly were doing. At times, those first days, Margaret's spare body seemed to expand to the size of a hot white giant, while she shrank as small as a baby. 'Don't you worry, I'll look after you,' Margaret had whispered, smiling, as if to do just that was exactly what she had always wanted.

They were finishing off the wine and lighting after-dinner cigarettes when the hall telephone rang. 'I expect it's for you.' His few friends were unlikely to call without reason, whereas Nelly's thought nothing of phoning from anywhere in the world for a gossip. 'Who was it?' he asked, disturbed by her expression.

'Margaret. She said they had a quarrel, and June hasn't come back. She wondered if she was here.' They tried to avoid mentioning June. There were awkward gaps in Nelly's stories; and after those days of excitement and confusion, when somehow he had convinced her that nothing could save the three of them from the most dreadful unhappiness for the rest of their lives except the immediate marriage of herself to him, Paul was careful about references to the last few years. 'Maybe she went for a walk to calm down, and is back already. If I ring in an hour or two she'll probably answer the phone herself.'

'Nelly, it's not your fault if the two of them quarrel. Margaret's just trying to make you feel guilty. Why did that evil woman phone and upset you?' He felt helpless and indignant. 'I know how much you've done for June. And I tried – ' He wished he could take her in his arms and laugh off the whole business, but something stopped him from moving.

'I suppose Margaret thought she should let us know.' Nelly's voice rose as she carried their coffee into the sitting-room and he followed behind. 'It's never happened before, darling, we must remember that. She sounded very worried.' She smiled wryly across the room from the chintz-covered sofa. 'Don't switch on the television.'

He understood that she was afraid to miss the sound of the phone ringing, the crunch of gravel as a car pulled up, or a knock at the front door. He glanced at his watch and could not believe it was only nine o'clock. 'Would you like a drink?'

'No thanks,' she answered without lifting her head. He closed the door behind him and went to the bedroom to dial the number of Margaret's Kilburn flat. The ringing tone went on and on but there was no reply. Baffled, he started down the stairs as the doorbell sounded. He almost collided with Nelly hurrying to answer it, then stood by her side as they watched the taxi pull away.

'What a lovely picture the two of you make, I must say. The newly-weds!' June wore dirty jeans and an old suede jacket. Her face was pale, eyes strained and red from the tears which had left smudges of mascara beneath them. Paul noticed this particularly; she never used to wear it. 'Aren't you going to invite me in? Mummy? And you – you're my stepfather now, aren't you? Shall I call you Daddy? Will I be Daddy's little darling?'

Nelly's arms lifted in a half-sketched embrace.

'Please don't start the loving-mother act. I've had enough of that to last a lifetime.'

'Well then, let's go and sit down.' Nelly's expression and movements were under control as they left the hall.

'I'll get you some coffee, June. We've had ours already.' He

116

had not expected to be so unnerved by seeing them together.

'Did Margaret phone?' She stretched out on the sofa, kicked off her shoes, and reached into a pocket for a crumpled packet of cigarettes.

Nelly watched her warily. 'I guessed you were on the way.'

'I'm not going back. I'm finished with her – I've had enough of all that.' She made a vague, inclusive gesture, then twisted on to her side and moaned, 'Why on earth did I come here?'

Nelly was stroking her hair when Paul returned. 'Anyone for coffee?' He felt so superfluous, so ridiculous, that he might as well make a joke of it.

June gave a shriek in which amusement, rage and despair struggled for primacy. 'This is the first time we've met since you jilted me, do you know that? It doesn't seem to have improved your sense of humour.'

'I kept expecting you to turn up at the wedding,' Nelly interrupted. 'Dreading it, to tell you the truth.'

It had been the wrong thing to say, she realised, watching June's face redden. 'Yes, that would have put the seal on it, proved to all and sundry how you just have to lift your finger and any man will come running, even your own daughter's boyfriend. Well, I'm sorry you didn't have your big scene.'

'Stop tormenting your mother.'

They both turned, astonished by his intervention.

'Yes, you heard me. If you're going to come to the house, you can't carry on like this.' Knowledge gained in past quarrels and reconciliations lay behind the look they exchanged.

'Really, Paul, June and I know what we mean when we talk to each other.'

'But maybe Paul doesn't. He's never had the privilege of watching us in action, has he?' June lit another cigarette. 'You didn't know what you were getting into.'

'Obviously not.' He took his usual seat by the fireplace filled with leaves and flowers Nelly had put there earlier in the day. 'Did you know that Margaret was in the habit of phoning your mother with progress reports?'

'She only rang a couple of times early on, when you weren't well. Naturally I was worried. But I hadn't heard from her for ages until tonight.' It was all happening too fast, Nelly thought. They relished it, but she struggled to keep afloat.

'What an underhand thing to do!'

'There was no need to tell her,' Nelly reproached him.

'Best to have everything out in the open.'

'So you and Margaret were plotting behind my back?'

'Of course not. I just wanted to know you were all right.'

'Taken care of, you mean. Less likely to bother you.'

'I wasn't trying to make trouble between you – or between you and Margaret, come to that.' Paul sounded as if he felt left out. 'But I thought you should know we'd been in touch.'

'I was hoping never to see either of you again.'

'I wish you'd accept what's happened, June. It's not as if we did it to hurt you.'

'Oh no, of course not. It was just bigger than both of you, one of the great love stories of the century!' Nelly and Paul lowered their eyes in embarrassment. 'I don't want to remember that time, it was too awful. I never thought either of you were capable of it. Paul and I were getting on all right.'

'You wanted me to look after you,' Paul said. 'To be what you kept calling "a real man" – '

'And then Nelly turned up and rescued you,' June scornfully finished his sentence. 'And you could go back to being a spoiled little make-believe writer.'

'That's it. You've admitted it.' He rose to his feet. 'You never believed in me. But Nelly – '

'But Nelly – ' she mimicked. 'Nelly thinks you're a genius! She doesn't know the first thing about it. You could believe in him,' June turned on her mother, 'but you never had faith in me.'

'That's not true,' Nelly contradicted, her tone unconvincing even to herself.

'You were never interested in me. You never thought I was good at anything, not at school, not afterwards. You wanted everyone to be interested in you. And then when I did manage to make a sort of life for myself at last, you had to take it away from me.'

'Will you both shut up!' Paul shouted.

The sleeping village and dark fields all around were like a force pressing inwards, reducing the significance of emotions and words, draining the energy necessary to continue. 'What's the use of all this talk?' Nelly said wearily. 'What's done is done.' In the silence they heard a dog bark, and the sound of an approaching car.

'If that's Margaret – ' June began.

'How on earth could she get here so quickly?' Paul muttered.

'Maybe she was already on her way when she phoned,' Nelly speculated.

'She can drive like the devil when she wants to. Anyway, I'm not going back with her, and that's definite.'

'It's Margaret all right,' Paul confirmed from the window. A car door slammed, and although prepared for it, each of them was startled by the loudness of the bell. 'Come in, we've been expecting you.'

'I guessed you'd be here,' she challenged June, paying no attention to the others.

'Well, you guessed right.'

Nelly stood up to greet her, face set in a conventional welcoming smile which Margaret did not seem to notice.

'There's no point following me,' June continued. 'I'm not going back with you. That's finished.'

'Let's not talk about it now. I don't suppose your mother and Paul want to listen to us squabble.'

'Don't be so mealy-mouthed. It's just like you to think they don't know what's going on.'

Margaret glanced uneasily towards them, trying to assess how much June had said.

'Perhaps you'd rather be left alone.' Nelly gave Paul a significant look.

'You don't have to go.' June's voice was imploring.

119

'Don't be silly, you'll be glad we did. Come on, Nelly.'

'Do you think they'll start hitting each other?' she giggled when they were in the hall.

'We've got enough trouble as it is, without having to administer first aid.' His flippancy rose to the level of hers. 'I wish we could go to bed . . . '

'What a marvellous idea. I'll be with you in a minute.'

He preferred to avoid the sight of Nelly's breasts – slack and loose against her ribcage, with large dark nipples. Whenever she made a remark she thought particularly amusing or perceptive, her chin lifted, her lips curled and pouted forward, and an expression of apprehensive delight gleamed from her eyes: a little girl waiting to be patted on the head by her Daddy for being such a clever darling. Paul stared up at the ceiling, dim in the partial light of the bed lamp, more disturbed by the contrast of ageing body and youthful, almost childish face than ever before. The silence from below was as oppressive as a lowering of atmospheric pressure.

Nelly felt excessively alert and wide awake. Paul was usually so loquacious after his wordless love-making that sometimes she dozed off during one of those monologues, and once or twice had wondered whether his idea of ultimate power over a woman was to talk her to sleep. But tonight he lay by her side saying nothing, his breathing as rapid and shallow as her own. Abruptly, he stood up, wrapped his dressing gown close, and only when about to leave the room turned to say, 'I think I'll go downstairs to make sure everything's all right.'

In a moment she was on her feet and tightening the belt of her own kimono. 'I'll come with you.'

Sighing heavily, he led the way. The sitting-room door was closed and nothing could be heard. They stood in the hall, uncertain what to do next.

'Well, I still want a drink,' Nelly insisted. Paul remained where he was. She came out of the kitchen carrying a tumbler of water, and after a quick knock vanished behind the sitting-room door. Pre-empted, he followed her example and retreated into the kitchen, where he tried to find something in the paper he hadn't yet read.

Margaret jumped up as the door opened, but a picture of her on the floor, head in June's lap and arms around her waist, impressed itself on Nelly's vision. 'I can't sleep,' she remarked in a high, bright voice, smiling in their general direction, and sat down in the nearest chair as if she had noticed nothing.

'Can't you leave me alone for a minute?' June was as indignant as if her earlier plea for support had never been made.

'I'm glad you're here. June's being so silly. I don't know why she says she doesn't want to come back to the flat.' Now it was Margaret who hoped for an ally.

'I've had enough of you, that's why. I'm sick to death of everything about you.'

The face Margaret turned towards her was so nakedly appalled that Nelly could not restrain her sympathy. 'You shouldn't be so harsh.'

'Whose side are you on? I told you I wouldn't go back with her, and I've told her, too – but it doesn't seem to do any good.' At that moment Paul entered the room and June ran to his side, threw her arms around his neck, and begged, 'You don't want to get rid of me, do you? You'll let me stay here and tell Margaret to go away, won't you?' Her cajoling yet desperate tone forced Margaret and Nelly to look at each other as if to confirm that what they heard and saw was really happening.

Paul carefully detached himself. 'Why don't you calm down? It's late, and we're all tired. Let's have a cup of tea – '

'A cup of tea! It's like a war movie. You should have been there in the Blitz, handing out cups of tea!'

'What else do you expect from me?'

'Now you're going to sulk. Oh, I know you. I remember it only too well.' She turned to the others with a broad gesture of hopelessness. 'It's like trying to explain something to a kid when you keep him in, and he doesn't listen, but just waits for you to stop talking so he can run off to his friends in the playground. I was a teacher for a while,' she explained to her mother. 'Or have you forgotten? That was when you were enjoying yourself somewhere, while I was doing what you called "making my own life".' The swathe of her recrimination had extended to include them all.

Nelly was the one who answered. 'So you want to stay here?'

It was only Margaret's eyes, fixed on him as though he had to be the strongest, which gave Paul the confidence to say, 'Come on, Nelly, let's go to bed. In the morning everything will look different.'

'I doubt it,' June muttered as they followed him upstairs.

Paul woke first, and as soon as he'd had something to eat and drink, put on his coat and went outside. He needed to be alone, and some hard exercise. After weeks of rain, it was a perfect spring morning. Pushing across fields which had been made inaccessible by Nelly's reluctance to get mud on her shoes, he suddenly thought that what he really wanted was to go away for a few days and let them do what they liked.

It was easy to be decisive now, but he feared his resolution would evaporate when he got back to the house. They were mother and daughter, after all – and if Nelly preferred June to him . . . He thrust the thought away, ashamed to let it develop. But every moment, his sense of being a free agent strengthened, and the excitement that feeling generated.

He stopped at the edge of a wood surrounded by barbed wire. The small new leaves glowed lime green in the sunlight, and the bluebells were luminous as neon against the sooty tree trunks. Money would not be a problem; Nelly had given him a cheque for a thousand pounds as a wedding present. And there were his own savings. He trudged back to the house, technicolor images of India, Italy, California, swirling through his mind.

Margaret was the next to appear. The unfamiliar bed had been lumpy and damp. She'd refused the proper guest room, insisting that June should sleep there, hoping to be invited to join her. But after Paul showed her the other little spare room and said goodnight, she had waited for a signal that never came. It was past three before she fell asleep, and dawn woke her again. The country silence was more disturbing than early morning traffic.

When she heard Paul leave the house, Margaret went down to the kitchen. Everything here looked new and expensive, evidence of Nelly's attempt to create an illusion of stability. She could not understand why this should seem so touching. Though the impulse was probably as mawkish and ridiculous as everything else about her this morning, she thought bitterly, she carried a tray of tea upstairs and hesitated outside Nelly's door before mustering the courage to knock.

Leaning back against a heap of pillows on one side of a low wide bed, and settling a fine cream-coloured Shetland shawl around her shoulders, Nelly stretched out a thin hand and arm. 'How kind.' There was an armchair near the window, where a net curtain softened the morning light. The room was full of white rugs, fragile-looking furniture, and small shining objects. 'Won't you sit down. We can drink our tea together.'

'I heard Paul go out,' Margaret said, after a pause.

'Yes. Do you know, he's never done that before? He's not been out for a walk on his own once since we came here. He always wants me to go with him. I've spoiled several pair of shoes.' She smiled slightly. 'I don't really enjoy walking in the country, but of course I went when he asked.'

'He and June used to walk a lot,' Margaret began, then stopped, feeling clumsier than ever.

'I think they have a great deal in common,' Nelly replied in a calm voice. 'I find June very persuasive as well.'

'What a lovely house this is.' Margaret tried to alter the direction of their conversation, but Nelly was determined to continue.

123

'I wanted to make a home for Paul where he could work at his writing. I think I have been trying to do for him what I should have done for June. It's hard to believe how easy it is to go on for so many years, doing all the wrong things.'

'I'm sure you haven't – ' Margaret protested.

'I know what I've done.' Nelly's voice was low but firm. She turned away and picked up the cup again. 'I think I'll get dressed now.'

'You've been in there a long time,' June called through her half-open door as Margaret passed. 'What were you talking about?' she demanded, face urgent with curiosity.

'Nothing special. I haven't seen that nightdress before.'

'I found it in the drawer. It's an old one of Nelly's.' The light seemed stronger here than in the other room. Already the sun was higher, and there were no net curtains to soften it. The frilled nightdress made June look about twelve years old, yet at the same time intensified the resemblance to her mother. Anger and yearning combined in a dizzying mixture. June's triumphant, self-assured expression made Margaret want to strangle her. 'I hope you're not falling under her spell like everyone else.'

'Don't worry, I'll be glad to get away from here. Are you coming with me or not?'

'How silly you look, glaring like that,' June remarked in a dreamy, provocative voice. 'Are you trying to frighten me?'

'I don't want to do anything to you,' she lied. 'I just thought you might like a lift back to town.'

'I'm quite capable of getting around on my own, thanks all the same. I'm not sure what my plans are.'

'What about your job – the flat? What's going to happen about all that?' She knew there was no point in mentioning herself.

'I'll take some sick leave.' June leaned back against the pillows, very much the daughter of the house – which made Margaret feel like the humble petitioner or the poor man at the gate – neither of which roles she could tolerate a moment longer. But she was unable to resist one final attempt.

'I didn't think it would end like this.'

'Neither did I,' June replied pertly. Margaret slammed the door and rushed out to her car. It was only after several miles that she remembered she had not said goodbye to Nelly.

Thank God for the Sunday papers, June thought, creeping back to bed with another cup of tea and the pile of supplements and colour magazines that had landed on the hall mat a few moments before. She heard Nelly move around her room and then descend to the ground floor. With Margaret gone, she hoped no one would disturb her for a while, though the possibility of being forgotten was unsettling. When Paul returned, although his and Nelly's voices were almost inaudible from the kitchen directly below, she could tell that a rapid and intense exchange was taking place.

'Margaret's car isn't outside.'

'She must have gone. Poor girl, I feel sorry for her. I got quite a different impression on the phone.'

'You'd better not tell that to June.'

'Not today, I agree.'

They were darting glances at each other through narrowed eyes, like wrestlers sizing up an opponent.

'She'll be all right. I'm always amazed by women's recuperative powers.'

'Yes,' she agreed vaguely, not yet ready to commence the bout. 'Did you have a nice walk?' She opened a cupboard door and closed it again.

'I was thinking about taking a trip,' he began, sitting down at the table.

'What a good idea!'

'I mean on my own.' He stared at his hands, loosely clasped together on the smooth wood.

'Ah, I see.' She chose a chair opposite him, and concentrated her gaze on the refrigerator.

Now that her face was averted he hunched forward as if about to begin a complicated and pleasurable discourse. 'It's wonderful what you've done for me, Nelly, to help me get on with my writing. But I feel I have to discover myself first.'

'I should have thought you'd done that already. You're not exactly on the threshold of manhood,' she said sardonically.

'Being here with you has made me feel I am.' He was too absorbed by his own words to notice their effect on her. 'I suppose it's because you've given me this chance to find out whether I really am a writer.'

'I was under the impression that you were.'

'I thought I was, too. But lately, I don't know – '

'Surely all you have to do is sit down and write?'

'That's easy for you to say!' He began to pace back and forth on his side of the room, as though it had been partitioned into two hostile territories. 'I thought you loved me because I'm myself, not because I'm a writer.'

'I thought the two were the same thing.'

'That's what I have to find out.'

'It's strange how you've only hit on this now – since June arrived.' Her direct appraisal made him furious..

'She has nothing to do with it.'

Nelly turned back to the refrigerator door.

'If you really did love me, you'd understand. You seemed to understand everything, not so long ago.'

She felt she was losing control of the conversation, that he was going to talk her into accepting an interpretation of his words which later she would discover was entirely opposed to her own. 'When do you want to go?' she asked abruptly.

He would have been perfectly happy to talk for hours. 'As soon as possible, I suppose. I can stay with Kenneth and make arrangements from there.' It was hard to believe that everything could end so quickly.

'Yes, of course. Much easier.'

126

There was a lot to be said for breeding, Paul thought, trying to hide his excitement. 'Well, let's have some coffee now, eh Nelly? Nothing's really changed, has it?' He put an arm around her. She was still a beautiful woman. He remembered that he was her husband and moved a hand on to the back of her neck.

The sudden memory of a hot-eyed uncle fondling her squirming six-year-old body, the lazy laughter of other uncles at the Sunday afternoon card-table and the smiling collusion of crocheting aunts, and her own helpless, excited resentment and fear, surged up from some deep-buried source. Paul was nothing like her uncle – but his proprietorial gesture somehow linked them, and if she could be true to herself now, that child might be vindicated. 'A great deal has changed, I think. You've just told me that you want to find yourself. Do you expect to find me still here when you decide to return?'

'But Nelly, you've got everything wrong. What I want to do is all part of being a writer.'

'Perhaps so – though it sounds nonsense to me. But while you're looking for yourself, what do you imagine I'll be doing?'

He had no answer. The well of persuasiveness had run dry.

'I know I can't stop you. You'll do what you want to. But you must understand that we shall be equally free.'

'What do you mean?' He did not seem able to take in what she was saying.

'Exactly what I say. Everything will be changed. We both have to accept that.' It was harder than she had expected, and she knew this feeling of impatience was caused by exhaustion as much as by disappointment, as though she had to deliver her message before she collapsed.

'We're still married to each other.'

Something in his tone made her blurt out, 'Then why don't you tell me you love me?' But as soon as the words left her mouth she knew that she had made a crucial mistake.

He concentrated on the decision already taken. 'I don't

127

know what's going to happen any more than you do. Things are more complicated than I thought. Of course I love you,' he added, guilty and impatient. 'But right now I have to get away.'

'Go then, do go, please.' She bowed her head on to the kitchen table. Paul went upstairs as though he were a thief in the house, crammed some clothes and his notebooks into two suitcases, and phoned the local garage for a taxi to the station.

As far as she could remember, she had never heard her mother cry. When her father died in that terrible accident, everyone had praised Nelly for not breaking down. Nelly had endured the condemnation and disapproval before this marriage with a stoical dignity, or indifference, that left June completely baffled and made any expression of her own feelings impossible. Always her mother had seemed strong and invulnerable – maddeningly so; there had never been a moment when June could imagine her as less than equal to every circumstance. Now, the prospect of seeing Nelly brought low was appalling; even more so, the overwhelming satisfaction she felt in the knowledge that it was Paul who had reduced her to this state.

Nelly's footsteps dragging up the stairs made her heart lurch with dread, then slow into relief and regret when they passed her door. A few moments later, as though released from a spell, she threw back the bedclothes and hurried across the landing. Nelly was bent over the washbasin, lifting cold water to her eyes, deafened by its splashing.

'Mother, are you all right?'

'Oh – June. I'd forgotten you were here.' Nelly reached for a towel to hide her face, trying to behave as though nothing were unusual.

'What's the matter, Mummy? What's happened? Where has Paul gone?'

'It's all right, it's all right,' Nelly repeated, features tensed into the rictus of a smile, while tears ran down her cheeks.

She pressed Nelly's head on to her own shoulder and felt the hot wetness through the nightdress and against her skin. 'There, there,' she crooned, leading her into the bedroom. 'Lie down, darling, let me take off your shoes. Here, I'll tuck the blanket around you.' She could not recall having enjoyed being with Nelly this much ever before.

If Nelly had been able to let June go on mothering her, perhaps everything would have been different. Afterwards, she understood that the only thing June had wanted then, for the first time in her life, was not to be the weaker one.

Impatiently pushing away the blanket she stood up, shuddering with the effort. To June, it seemed as though she shuddered with repulsion at her touch.

'How can you hate me so much?' She spoke in a low voice, instinctively taking a step backwards and lifting one hand to press it against her chest. 'Is it so much worse to have me touch you than anyone else?'

Nelly stared blankly for a moment, then realised what June meant. 'June darling, don't torment me now. Of course I don't hate you.' That was as much as she could manage.

'Paul's done it, hasn't he? He's the one who's made you so unhappy.'

'He's gone away for a while.'

June's face assumed a gleeful, cunning expression, like an old woman on the verge of senility. 'Now you know how I felt! Not nice, is it? Serves you right. I'm glad.'

It was like being slapped across the mouth. But there was a new aspect to her daughter which pushed her own troubles to one side. 'No, it's not nice at all. But let's not talk about it now. Let's go downstairs and have a cup of coffee. Aren't you cold, darling? Here, I'll wrap my shawl around you.'

'Yes, Mummy.' June's voice was clear and docile. She moved closer and took Nelly's hand. It was raining again, but later, Nelly holding an umbrella over their heads while June held her mother's arm, the two of them went out for a walk to the river, on the road that passed the farm.

THREE AMBIGUOUS VISITORS

Susan leaned on one elbow and smiled down at him, happy to see that at such a moment he still could present the smooth, mysterious, young man's face that had fascinated her twenty years before. The sheet was thrown back, and clothes scattered where they had dropped, as though they were lovers meeting secretly and rarely, rather than a married couple. 'It's completely different, being alone in the house. It reminds me of before we had the children.'

'Yes,' he laughed, half-rueful. 'I usually expect one of them to wander through the door. Not at all the same.' He turned to embrace her again.

A window rattled in the wind, but otherwise, everything was quiet. The house stood in its deep garden on the edge of the village, and after sundown there was rarely any traffic along the lane which led to a few isolated farms. Rising to low hills on all sides, the valley was populated mainly by sheep and a column of electric pylons. The only sound which might disturb them was the crackle of gunfire when there was a rabbit shoot, or during the hunting season.

She was not so absorbed now, and over his shoulder watched the curtain sucked back and forth against the half-open window, a corner of the bed reflected in the wardrobe mirror, and the variegated textures of wallpaper, fabrics and glass. She saw the door opening, but no sound until then had alerted her to the fact that someone else was in the house.

'Peter!' she gasped, as the gap widened and the three men came in. They were almost at the side of the bed before he realised what her cry meant, and had rolled away to pull the sheet over them both, sit upright and glare at the intruders, in one panicky gesture.

'That was very nice,' the nearest man said. 'Sorry we had to disturb you.' He was smiling, but the other two seemed to find nothing in the situation that demanded a response. Susan lay without moving, head reared up as if trying to stretch as far from her body as possible. The three of them gazed calmly back. They appeared to be in their twenties, a bit older than Peter's students at the university.

Peter reached to the bed table for his glasses. 'What are you doing in my house?'

'Don't worry, we won't harm you if you do what we say,' the same man who had spoken before replied. He had the thin face and smooth, dull white skin of a cleric. Dark hair fell to the shoulders of a blue denim jacket which, in combination with blue jeans, made him seem to be in uniform. The others wore similar clothes, and carried small haversacks on their backs. 'Just don't try anything ridiculous.'

'You can't walk in here and start ordering me about – '

'My name is Jim.' He ignored the interruption. 'Don't think my friends and I are thieves. You needn't worry, all your carefully chosen possessions are quite safe – for the moment, anyway. We just want to stay here a while.'

'What have your friends got in those bags? Is it explosives?'

The blond man shrugged his pack off and dropped it carelessly in a corner by the door. 'You've been reading the papers.'

'Is there anyone else in the house?'

Susan carefully raised an arm to smooth her short light hair. 'No. The children are away. And a good thing, too.'

'I don't know,' Jim said thoughtfully. 'Kids are better than grown-ups, quicker on the uptake. They're more reliable. They know what's happening and what has to be done. No, we don't have half so much trouble with the kids as with their parents. They understand us.'

'I want to get up,' Peter said. 'Go outside so we can dress.'

'Why be so modest? Dress if you want to. Then you can come downstairs and make us a cup of tea. I don't know about the others, but I'm thirsty.'

Peter stepped sideways from the bed, making sure he did not uncover his wife and that his stomach was sucked in so he would appear at his best before these men half his age. He was not as frightened now, but nevertheless, did not turn his back on them for one moment while pulling on shirt and trousers.

'Do you have any guns in the house?' Jim leaned against the wardrobe door, arms folded across his chest. He looked tired, or preoccupied.

'Do we seem the hunting type?' Susan asked.

'I haven't the slightest idea about that,' he replied stiffly. 'But it would be quite normal to have a gun these days. Even rather sensible, don't you think?'

She flushed as if insulted. 'Well, we haven't got one.'

'Tony, look around, will you?' He mumbled an assent and started to pull out drawers and feel through their contents.

'Didn't you believe me?'

The fair man shook his head sadly.

'Is there a phone up here?' Jim asked.

'Out in the hall,' Peter nodded. 'One there, and one downstairs in the kitchen.'

'You'd better stay by the one up here, Tony, while she gets dressed. We'll go down with him and have something to eat.'

When Susan entered the kitchen, followed by her silent guard, she found them drinking tea and cutting up a loaf of bread and slab of cheese at the long wooden table.

'Shall I pour you some?' Jim asked.

'This isn't a tea-party, you know. You've broken into our house, and now you're offering me a cup of tea. It's ridiculous.'

'It's good tea.'

'Have a cup, Susan.' Anger suited her, and Peter hoped that Jim would be equally charmed by her heightened colour and flashing eyes.

She glared at her husband. 'We shouldn't be sitting here with them as if they're weekend visitors. I want to know what's happening.' She ignored the proffered cup.

'Why don't you act as if we are? It would be much easier. We don't want to get you mixed up in this. We came into your house because we had to get out of sight for the moment.'

'You mean someone's looking for you?'

'You could say that. We're not here, as far as anyone is ever going to know. I want you to get that quite clear. If there are any enquiries, you don't know a thing. No one came, and you haven't seen or heard anything.'

Peter stared across the table, willing her to agree and not cause trouble. The fact that there was nothing they could do about this situation, not even talk about it together, made her dizzy with helplessness. For a moment she was too angry even to be frightened, but then she became aware of the other two men, hunched and alert, prepared for any unexpected move. It was serious, she understood, sitting down at last, conscious of wanting that cup of tea.

'Is anyone expected tomorrow morning? One of the local council-house ladies to do the charring? I suppose you do live that way, don't you?' Jim's voice was contemptuous. As well as all her other feelings, Susan became aware of a surge of self-justification.

'Yes, I do have a charlady – and I need one, too, with this big house and the family and everything.'

'Shouldn't have such a big house, then,' the blond man intervened. 'There's room for two or three families by the look of it. It's wrong to have so much space. And people should clean up their own messes and dirt, not exploit economic need.'

'Tony never misses a chance to start discussing theory,' Jim laughed. 'No use trying to make a convert, Tony.'

'Just saying what I think.' He bent his head to take another sip of tea.

'Well, what time does she come in?'

'She's having her holiday. I do let her have a holiday, you know. I'm not such a dreadful exploiter.'

'You've got to, haven't you?' He did not bother to look up.

'No one's coming in.' She felt defeated. 'The kids are away, she's on holiday – you couldn't have chosen a better time.'

'What about you?' Jim turned to Peter. 'What time do you go out to work?'

'I'm not going out tomorrow,' he replied ingratiatingly. 'I'm a university lecturer. All my students are on holiday, and I suppose I am as well – though I'm working on a book.'

'That sounds like a good job.' The third man spoke for the first time. His voice lacked the precise, educated tones of the others. 'Better than a couple of weeks off a year.'

'Yes, I suppose it is.' Peter tried to disguise his nervous titter with a cough, but began to choke in earnest, sweat breaking out on his face and half-bald head.

'You certainly take a very moral attitude. What gives you the right to be so superior?' Susan glared from one to the other. 'You don't know anything about us at all.'

'Only what you're telling us,' Jim replied. 'But that's quite a lot, and looking around helps. I'm sure you think you're extremely enlightened, so you needn't bother to establish your credentials. They're littered all over the place. I'll bet you've even got *Private Eye* and *The New Statesman* in the toilet.'

'Would you feel better if it were the *Field* or the *Tatler*?' She was stung by the accuracy of his assessment.

'It wouldn't make much difference in the long run. Maybe we wouldn't have to talk so much, or maybe we'd even hear something a bit less predictable.'

The church clock began to thud its twelve midnight strokes. No one in the large kitchen moved until they had finished, and the silence which followed seemed even more oppressive.

'It's a quiet place here, all right,' Tony remarked. 'I don't know if I'd like it or if it would drive me crazy.'

'I'm done in,' the other man said. 'Let's get some sleep.' But instead of acting on these words, he took out a packet of cigarettes. 'Any of you want one?'

'I gave it up a couple of years ago,' Peter replied.

'Thanks.' She wanted to go on talking. 'What's your name?'

'Bill. What do you want to know for, anyway?' He had wavy, chestnut hair, and the roughness of his skin and fullness of his face made him appear the youngest.

'Is this a regular activity for the three of you? Breaking into people's houses late at night, I mean, and not explaining what you want or who you are? Have you been doing it a long time? I suppose they talked you into it. It must be fun.'

'It's no good trying to get anything out of him,' Jim interrupted. 'Or us, either. The less you know, the better.'

'I think he's right,' Peter joined in. 'I'm not interested in what they're doing. I just hope they won't cause any damage or do us any harm.'

If only he hadn't said that. She was ashamed of him. His words reminded her of what she had been glad to forget for a few minutes. During those exchanges she had felt reasonably confident, but now she was forced to remember how much they were at the mercy of the others.

Jim seemed amused. 'Well, we weren't planning to shit on your carpets. I hear it's standard practice in some circles.' When he noticed her shock, the expression of pleasure in conveying this useful information – as though his true nature was that of a pedagogue – became more calculating and malicious. 'You must be pretty uneasy about what we could do, all alone here. There's no reason why we shouldn't torture you both to death just for the fun of it, is there?'

Susan and Peter involuntarily glanced towards each other for support.

'You don't strike me as being that sort of person.' Peter's voice rose hopefully at the end of the sentence.

'Or we could all have a bash at your wife. That would be more in the order of things, and not really harmful, either, would it? After all, she's a big girl, and it wouldn't cause any permanent damage.'

He was just playing with them, trying to break their nerve. She hoped this interpretation was correct. She could feel her skin prickle, adrenalin like a thump in the solar plexus, her heart speed up and her breath shorten. She tried to conceal any outward sign of these reactions, as though they were wild dogs who would be bound to attack once they sensed her fear.

'Don't worry, love,' Bill cut in. 'We're not going to do any of it. Speaking for myself, I'm whacked. We must have walked twenty miles today. I just want to flake out.'

'All right. OK.' Jim shook his head a few times in a baffled manner, as though displacing a cloud of midges. 'There's so much sick stuff around, it gets you by the throat before you know what's happening. Yes, we're tired. We'll have to take it in turns to guard you, though. Come on, show them where they can lie down, and I'll take the first watch.'

Now it was herself Susan felt ashamed of, alarmed by. Her imagination had raced ahead of his words and, by anticipating atrocity, in another situation might have tipped the balance towards it. She took them to the spare room, where there were two single beds, stripped to the pattern of the mattress ticking. 'I'll get some sheets.'

'Don't bother, we won't undress. A blanket each will do.'

The blankets were in a chest in the room. She looked around, eyes alert and competent, once more for a moment mistress of the house. 'You can turn the light out from there. And there's a bathroom across the hall.'

Tony began to unlace his boots. 'I'll come down next, Jim, OK? Then Bill can do the last stint.'

'Fine. Now, where are we going to be?'

She certainly would not go back to the bedroom with him, and in any case felt too overwrought to sleep. 'What about the sitting room?' she asked Peter.

'I was thinking of going back to bed.'

'We can stretch out on the couches if we want to.'

Peter went first, switching on the central light. Close behind him, Susan put on the smaller lamps, then went back to the door to turn off the overhead one. 'You know I think it's more restful like this.' She drew the curtains.

Jim observed this marital ritual with astonishment, but made no comment. He chose an armchair under the standard lamp, then drew a folder from his haversack and extracted several sheets of paper. Peter and Susan sat side by side on the couch, staring anxiously first at each other and then towards him, uncertain whether they would be allowed to converse. Jim looked up. 'How far are you from a railway station?'

'Six miles. That's the branch line. The main line passes about fifteen miles away.'

'Not too close, is it? I suppose you go by car?'

'Yes.' Peter leaned forward, eager and curious, but the other man did not say anything else, and after a few minutes he slumped back. 'Say,' he called across to Jim. 'Do you mind if I go for a pee?'

In spite of Peter's denials of any intention to run out into the night, Jim insisted that he and Susan accompany him to the downstairs cloakroom.

'Why don't you tell us what you're doing?' Susan asked when they were back in the sitting-room 'We can't get away, so it doesn't matter. We might even be able to help.'

'I doubt it. Just keep quiet and don't think about using your initiative or trying any other bourgeois heroics, and everything will go smoothly. We don't want any trouble, but it's up to you.'

Peter lay down on the chaise-longue and fell asleep at once. Susan had already imagined a thousand different stories to explain the arrival of the three men, and longed to know how close she had come to the real one. She was maddened by Jim's total absorption. She cleared her throat, smiled in his direction, stood up and then sat down again. But Jim went on making marks as if checking some sort of list, and ignored her. She walked across the room to take a book from the shelf behind him, then bent over the back of his chair.

He snapped the papers over and twisted round. 'Clear off.'

'I thought I could do something to help – ' She flinched from the malevolence in his face and voice.

He let the folder slide on to the floor, and with one rapid movement pulled her across his lap. 'You're more stupid than I thought. I suppose you imagine some romantic drama with yourself as the heroine – your mind must be crammed with that sort of disgusting fantasy. You're probably disappointed we didn't rape you.' He thrust a hard cold hand down the front of her jeans. 'Is this what you want?'

She struggled away, gasping with shock and excitement.

'You don't even care that your husband's in the room. It probably turns you on.'

If Peter were to wake and see them, anything might happen. She slowly got to her feet.

'Women like you disgust me.' He rubbed the hand that had touched her back and forth against the leg of his trousers, as if it were contaminated. 'You'll let anyone do what they like to you, as long as you can tell yourself you're not responsible, and that it's an adventure. Now get back over there.'

She was lucky to have been brought to her senses so quickly, she thought, conscious of the shamed flush mantling her throat and face. After all, he was nothing but a thug. How could she have imagined even for an instant that she might be accepted by them, and that this incident might totally change her life? She stalked across to the empty couch, stretched out and bent her head into its stuffy corner, remembering times she had tried to get to sleep on an overnight train journey. She was vaguely aware of Tony coming into the room and Jim's departure, but only woke properly to the sound of curtains being drawn back and the sudden intensity of daylight which made her sit up, look around, and realise where she was and what had happened.

Bill was on guard now, and Peter was not in the room. 'Where's my husband?'

'Oh, he's in the kitchen with the others. I stayed here so you wouldn't be lonely, see?' She couldn't tell if he was mocking or trying to be friendly.

She called 'Good morning' from the doorway. They looked up for a moment, then returned to their scrutiny of the map spread out on the table. Peter seemed no different from the others. He didn't give her a special reassuring smile or make any movement towards her. Perhaps he was the one who would leave with them, she thought, more agitated by that possibility than by anything since their arrival.

'Why don't you cook some breakfast, darling? I know we've got plenty of eggs and bacon, because I did the shopping yesterday. A good thing too, eh?' He was so pleased with himself that all her protective responses were mustered when she noticed Jim's amused expression. If he was enjoying himself playing revolutionaries, she would do whatever was necessary to sustain the illusion.

Bill wiped his plate with a piece of bread. 'That was great.'

'You can say that again,' Tony added.

'I wish you'd tell me more,' Peter asked. 'I'm really interested. Don't assume I'd disagree with you.'

Jim's rejecting manner had softened. 'If they find we've been here – though I don't see how they can if my plan works out – it's much better if you don't seem too knowledgeable or sympathetic. They might think you're involved, they're stupid enough for anything. It wouldn't do you any good, believe me.'

'I'm sure he's right, Peter.' She felt realistic and hard-bitten and down to earth, older than any of them.

'She *is* right,' Tony confirmed. 'She's got common sense.' But even before his speech, Susan knew that the four men had dismissed her from their minds.

'I'm still tired,' Jim said. 'I think we should take turns

sleeping today, it's too good an opportunity to miss. One of us will have to stay with you, of course.'

To Susan's surprise, Peter chose to move into his study. 'I might as well get on with my work,' he explained, picking up some papers on the desk. 'This has given me some good ideas, and I don't want to forget them. Oh, nothing connected with you,' he reassured Jim. 'It's this book I'm doing.' He stooped over his notes, and began to write even before sitting down.

'I suppose I'll read,' Susan remarked to no one in particular. Peter had stopped talking to her about his work years ago. Jim held a small, powerful-looking radio. 'This shouldn't disturb you, I've got headphones.' He slumped against the wall, eyes glazed. She had no idea whether he was listening to pop music, a symphony concert or the police reports. Through the window she stared at her garden as if watching a film unroll. It was a perfect late summer day. She knew there was no point in suggesting that they go outside.

'All right, dear?' Peter looked up from his papers with an absent-minded smile after an hour or so.

'Of course,' she said wryly. 'By the way, would you like some coffee?' Even to act as their serving maid would be more satisfying than this present nullity.

The afternoon crumbled away. No one called or phoned. As the house threw its shadow further out across the lawn, and the sky became more golden, a change of mood came over their three gaolers – or visitors – or comrades; Susan was no longer sure how she regarded them. Even her resentment of Jim had dissolved. It seemed as if they had all been in the house for ever, and that nothing could be more natural than this present style of life. They were checking their haversacks, taking things out and repacking them more neatly and securely – extra socks, T-shirts, notebooks: what anyone might have when camping.

'Shall I get some food ready for you?' she asked. They reminded her of friends of her children, about to set out on an expedition.

Peter offered to make sandwiches.

The three men looked at each other. 'Won't it be a lot of trouble?' Tony asked.

'Of course not. And why don't you have a bowl of soup or something hot before you go?' She suspected that he was trying to postpone the moment when they would be left alone together.

It was like an evening years ago, when she and Peter were students. They ate soup and bread, drank coffee, and laughed a lot. The tension had gone, as well as the distinction between guard and prisoner. When the meal was finished, Jim and Bill and Tony moved into the far corner of the kitchen for a final consultation.

'Well, thanks for everything,' Jim said.

'You've been great,' the others agreed.

'Good luck,' Peter called softly, as they slipped through the kitchen door into the blackness of the garden. He closed and locked it, head bent thoughtfully towards his chest.

'I feel exhausted. I don't know about you, but I'm going straight to bed.'

I must be stunned, Susan thought, unable to tell whether she was relieved or furious, if she would stay awake for the rest of the night or fall asleep immediately.

Without saying anything further they went upstairs. The house felt even bigger and emptier than when the children had left. Their bed was still disordered from the previous night. She pulled the sheets and blanket up and undressed. When Peter put his arms around her, she began to cry. In a few minutes the sobs became tiny helpless giggles. He stroked her shoulders and back, trying to soothe her.

Suddenly, she clutched him. 'Listen,' she said. 'I'm sure I can hear shooting out there.'

IV

THE FISH-SCALE SHIRT

The wooden trough where she stood to work was darkened and spongy from a constant flow of water that poured out at an odd twisted angle – like an icicle at the corner of a roof – through a large brass tap fixed on to the wall of the boat shed, and the ground below the trough was always slimy. Moss took hold wherever it could, though there were few places not sealed against its advance by a glistening varnish of fish scales, which gave the scene a paradoxical elegance, as if the barrels and buckets, the baskets into which the cleaned fish were packed, the trough and puddled yard and collapsing huts and fences that surrounded it, were inlaid with mother-of-pearl. Ann saw and thought about fish scales all day, dreamed of them every night. Her task was to collect enough to cover the shirt she had to make. She tried to imagine how it would look: a glittering shirt of fish-scale sequins, like chain-mail armour.

She had woken one morning on the shore of a small harbour, where fishing boats rose and sank at the horizon with the timeless regularity of waves breaking on a stony beach. Someone must have brought her there, but she had no memory of the journey. The contrast with her previous life was so decisive that she might as well have been shot into space and landed on another planet. An old woman had appeared at her side and given details of the task, adding that when the garment was ready, Ann would discover who it was intended for. She could never find that woman again among the others.

With them, each day she split and gutted the gleaming bodies tumbled from weed-tangled, barnacle-crusted nets on to the cobbled quayside. The skill and speed of her workmates was astonishing. She watched carefully, trying to see how they managed to open and clean a large fish in what seemed one flowing movement. Her chapped hands and fingers, covered with small cuts, smarted from the cold air and salt water. These strong-limbed, full-bodied women, and the tall fair sailors in sea boots and oilskins who looked like their brothers and husbands, joked together all day long – shining teeth and glistening lips and tongues in noisy action to speak a dialect she could barely comprehend. But in spite of their energetic, friendly presences, they stayed as unreal to her as she must be to them. Nevertheless, she studied the men's faces and gestures, and listened to their different tones of voice, seeking a sign that this or that one might become the wearer of the fish-scale shirt. A few had made tentative yet unmistakable approaches, but they soon stopped when she did not respond. None had the special quality that marked a prince in disguise.

The old woman had shown Ann a broken-down lean-to behind the fish sheds, and said that was where she would live. There was a pile of sacks inside, which she took to the beach and washed in the foam. It was a windy, sunny day and they dried quickly, spread over clumps of seaspurge and marram grass. They would serve for blanket and towel and pillow. She also found a tin plate, a chipped enamel bowl and mug, and a sharp knife. One of the fisherwomen gestured her to come and share their round loaves of bread and cauldron of fish soup. Her basic needs were provided. At the end of a day's hard work and the communal meal, Ann fell on to the bed of sacks as if it were the most luxurious divan and slept more deeply than she could remember ever having done before.

How to gather the fish scales was the first problem. If her hands and arms were wet from fish juices and sea water, they clung to her skin, impossible to detach. They seemed as fragile and easily damaged as the scales on butterflies' wings. If her hands were stiff from gripping the hard bone handle of the knife and the icy bodies of the dying fish, the scales slid through her clumsy fingers. By trial and error she learned that the best way to gather the scales was to let them dry where they landed, then come back and gently scrape them off with the blunt edge of the knife into the lap of her skirt. It was a slow method, but she could not think of a better one. Day by day, the heap of scales in the corner of the hut mounted higher.

Having decided that none of the fishermen was an enchanted prince the fish-scale shirt would release (so that he in his turn could rescue her), Ann looked at the women more closely. There was no reason why her hero might not be a heroine. But although each in her own way was amiable, neither did any of them convince her as the destined one.

'When the time comes, your hero will appear,' a voice half sang and half intoned, inside her head. 'Just go on doing what you must, gathering the fish scales, and thinking about how to make the shirt to sew them on, and what you will use for needle and thread.' The voice was her companion. There was something familiar and reassuring about it, like a reminder of childhood. But whether the voice was that of mother or father or nurse or someone else, she could not be sure – nor even if it was her own.

Now the problem had been stated, it did not seem so daunting. She could make a needle from a strong straight fishbone, and pierce an eye through its thicker end with the point of her knife. Splitting open the firm cold bodies and scraping them clean, she wondered if she could use the silvery intestines for thread. But the shrivelled, hardened state of some she had put aside overnight eliminated that possibility.

Every day, cold winds beat rain on to the stone quay and high massed clouds moved steadily across the sky. But between the squalls, sunlight lit their edges with vivid silver and flashed from the encrustations of mica-fine fish scales. On certain evenings the sunset melted crimson, orange and purple bands into the horizon. Either the season was softening, or else she was adjusting to the climate's harshness. One morning, picking up a sacking blanket she had thrown off during the night, it became obvious how the shirt could be made and where the thread would come from. Such practical matters left no time to grieve about her past life or this one. She carefully frayed the rough fabric into the shape of a shirt-body and sleeves, then teased out separate threads to stitch seams down the sides and around the edges. 'I hope my hero won't be too tall or broad,' she mused, holding it against herself. The shirt was hardly larger than her own.

The next step was to sew on the scales, one stitch for each, in overlapping rows. Now the days were longer, rays of sunlight struck through the open door of the hut to the far corner, where the glittering heap dazzled like tidewater over wet bright stones along the shoreline. The slightest current of air would lift a few to skid across the floor or fly upwards then settle on her head like snowflakes or apple blossom. Hunched over a dim, but pungent, fish-oil lamp, she continued working until dawn made the lamplight even weaker. The nearer she came to finishing the shirt, the more Ann wondered why she had been set this task.

One day she walked further inland than ever before. Smooth, blackish rocks were scattered on the dark ground – isolated boulders or massive stones piled like cairns built by giants. She noticed a wisp of steam at the base of one where an overhanging shelf of rock sloped back into the earth. Between two black stone lips a hot spring bubbled up in sudden irregular gouts like blood being pumped from a deep wound. Grey scum, brilliant green moss and thick white mineral streaks rimmed the outlet in the shape of something being born from the cleft in the rocks.

The sense of another presence and a movement to one side made Ann turn her head, to be confronted by the speckled yellow eyes and unblinking gaze of a large brown toad sheltering there. This must be the one she had been waiting for, she thought excitedly, the one who had waited here for her. Only a creature under a spell would be in this magical place. And the toad was so repulsive that it must surely change into the handsomest prince in the world.

She smiled encouragingly and reached out to touch its head, but at the last moment could not make herself do so. She hoped the toad had not noticed this hesitation, and would not be offended or angry or hurt. Walking slowly backwards she chanted, 'Come home with me, dear toad-prince. Come to my hut. Come and see what I am making for you.' And heaving itself forward with an unpleasant movement and a sound like a paper bag full of water being bumped across a wooden floor, the toad followed. Every few steps she turned to make sure it was still there, and each time the toad stared back with a more intense, significant and intelligent expression.

She must be right to believe the toad was an enchanted prince. No ordinary toad would be so delicate, so considerate. All the stories she remembered about princesses forced to be goosegirls, or take a vow of silence and live in a tree spinning thread from nettles, or sorting every poppy seed from an enormous heap of lentils and pebbles ended happily in a transformation scene. By comparison to such tasks, hers was not really hard – and she might have made it easier, she realised, by being more friendly with her workmates and the fishermen. But that would have meant abandoning all hope in the redemptive power of her ordeal, and accepting this existence as permanent.

She had been uneasy about what he might expect, but the toad barely stirred from his place in the furthest corner of the hut, opposite the diminishing pile of fish scales. Ann's first thought when she woke was of him, and her first act was to confirm that the squat warty creature was still there, and meet his insistent yellow stare. She began to appreciate the variations of tone on his mottled back. Her life was different now she knew he would be waiting in the hut at the end of each day. She had no idea how he fed himself. The first few evenings she had brought back some soup in an old bowl and put it down in front of him, but the food remained untouched. She supposed he went outside to drink water and catch flies or whatever else toads eat, while she was at the harbour.

She had sewn the final overlapping row of scales, knotted and bitten off the last length of thread, and held the garment out for them both to admire. The toad seemed to examine it with great interest. Ann thought she might faint from the excitement. She moved closer and lifted the shirt high above his head, while she imagined a handsome young man uncoiling from the ungainly body and rising up to meet the garment in mid-air as it settled on to his wide, smooth shoulders. But in the instant between her letting go and its collapse on to the dirt floor, the toad hopped away into the furthest corner.

She picked up the shirt and shook the creases out. Some of the scales had been bent to one side and a few had fallen off, but it still looked extraordinary – glinting like metal yet as delicate as soap bubbles. 'Don't hop away, dear prince,' she murmured, carefully taking the shirt by the seam of each shoulder and raising it above him once more. He had already flexed his back legs in preparation for a leap before she moved, so the shirt did not fall on to the ground again. 'Toad, toad, don't you want to be a prince?' she asked, half laughing with vexation. The toad was as silent as ever.

After several more attempts at investiture and spell-breaking, Ann had to accept either that her prince preferred to remain a toad, or else was and never had been anything except a simple natural creature. She opened the door and it hopped out and disappeared into the darkness. She held the shirt up in front of her own eyes and regarded it ruefully.

She was the one who had been enchanted, in thrall. The shirt was beautiful. She remembered that there had only been enough sacking to make a small one and that it should certainly fit. She pulled it over her head and walked through the open door. Perhaps she had felt a comparable joy and freedom years before, but this seemed quite unlike anything she could recall. The fishwives and fishermen were drinking and laughing on the quay. She smiled and they smiled back and waved as she strode past. Quite soon she came to a broad highway behind the rise of the land. A silvery car, reflecting the moonlight like the fishscales on her shirt, stood waiting – door unlocked, key inside. She sat down behind the wheel and drove south.

MY LITTLE SISTER

My little sister came into the room and saw the blood on my throat. Her dark eyes opened wide with fear and uncertainty, her dark wavy hair slid backwards over the shoulder of her red dress as she turned first in my direction, as though to confirm that such a sight could be true, then to Oswald. One could see the questions forming behind the translucent skin of her temples and brow. How was it possible that I, her mentor and guardian, should be lying stretched out on the sofa, blood welling from a bite high up on the side of my neck, while Oswald bent over me, either as though examining the wound or perhaps having just inflicted it, and yet for us both to be smiling and laughing?

'Shall I go away?' she asked, stepping backwards and stretching one hand behind her as though groping for the doorknob. 'Are you all right?' she asked, swaying forward, torn between impulses to help and to flee.

Oswald took a crumpled handkerchief from the pocket of his black jacket. 'Press this against your neck, it's still bleeding,' he said. I could see him try to change the expression on his dark narrow face, to deny the impression of frivolity we must have created.

'It's all right, darling.' I sat up and gestured her towards me. 'It's nothing. You go and get a bowl of warm water, Oswald, so I can bathe it.'

I was accustomed to Oswald's sudden cruel actions. Under

my long skirts and sleeves were bruises from unexpected tweaks and pinches, healing half-scabbed scratches from his nails, or cuts where he had plunged the narrow sharp blade of his pocket knife. Sometimes I could sense, with a resigned, almost exalted prescience, when he was going to hurt me; accepted it as part of his strangeness, a sign of his love. But until this moment, though the three of us had been alone in the house for a long time, I had managed to hide such evidence from her. At twelve, she was too young to question Oswald's presence, yet observing how stiffly she sat on the extreme edge of the sofa and examined me with a dubious, almost pathetic expression, I realised that the time had come to give some explanation.

'Oswald is very fond of us both, Julia darling,' I began. 'He is our only friend, and I love him. We love each other.' I could see that her gaze was held by the bloodstained handkerchief still pressed against my neck. 'Don't be worried by that. It was just a love-bite.' I could not help smiling as I said those words. Staring intently into my eyes, Julia took her cue from me, and a timid smile began to lift the corners of her mouth. I leaned forward to hug her. The handkerchief dropped on to the floor, but the blood on my neck had already congealed. 'I love Oswald, but I love you most of all.'

Her dear head pressed against my shoulder, her slight arms circled my waist. I was more than twice her age, and since our parents' deaths in that terrible accident which ended my youth and banished us to this lonely house at the other side of the country, I had loved her like my own child. Now she could not see my face, its hard-maintained reassuring expression altered as I stared unseeingly into the dim corners of the shabby room wondering how I could protect her.

I did not want Julia to associate love with the malice and cruelty which characterised Oswald's behaviour, even if I chose to. Oswald had appeared one day, looked at me in a certain way, and since then could do whatever he liked with me. I still found it hard to understand how at the same time it was possible to recognise his tricks and yet succumb to them; but had to accept that such was the case. I knew that Oswald was wasting my fast-diminishing inheritance – mine and Julia's, to be exact; that he was capricious and extravagant; that he was neither polite, well-educated nor attractive and, I suspected, would be incapable of sustaining himself in the outside world. When I had asked about his previous life, he refused to answer. I knew that our lonely house was his refuge, and that because of him, no one in the district would have anything to do with us. I was by no means convinced that he loved me. I knew that when he arched his back and drew himself up, eyes almost closed under raised brows as he assumed his passionate glare, he looked quite ridiculous – and yet that particular look always worked, and I despised myself because it did. It was like becoming a lower life-form, existing below the level of will and self-respect and individual responsibility. He gave me such pleasure that the price exacted in pain seemed justified in some cosmic balance. But this was no reason for Julia to be involved in the transaction. So when Oswald returned, his close-cropped, almost furry dark head bent over the bowl of hot water, it seemed very important that Julia should see him care for me.

Conforming to this wish as if he read my mind, Oswald carefully swabbed and dried the laceration. Unless certain that his intention was sexual, I felt uneasy when he came too close. Without its mask of domineering arrogance, his face did not please me. Imagining a meeting in more normal circumstances, I knew that, dressed in his tight, stained black suit and muddy boots like the misfit son of a land worker, I would have thought him peculiar and even stupid-looking.

'Take the bowl away, Julia,' he ordered. 'Throw it outside.' Rain drove against the long windows, but Julia was used to being alone in the house or outside in the neglected grounds for hours at a time. Oswald had forbidden me to send her to school, and she and I never left the estate. He was the one who went into the village to buy provisions or do whatever was necessary, even helping with heavy work around the house rather than let me have anyone come in.

As soon as Julia was out of the room, Oswald squeezed my breasts and his thin mouth widened with glee. 'Well, things have changed, haven't they? She knows about us now – everything will be different.'

'I want you to be nice.' I tried to keep a pleading note out of my voice. 'I want Julia to see how nice you are. I want her to know what love can be.'

'Oh, I'll show her what love is really like,' he answered. 'You're quite right. It's time she learned. Just wait a minute, I'll get things ready.'

I closed the curtains and lit the lamps. Perhaps it would be better if Julia went straight to bed. But as if in response to this thought she walked back into the room and across to the chimney, where she stretched out her hands to its warmth.

'Do you feel all right, Mary dear?' Her large eyes were lustrous in the firelight.

'It was nothing – look, it's almost better.' She stroked the side of my face and then my hair, as long as hers but fairer, as we silently watched the flames.

Oswald pushed through the door, arms laden with firewood, then hurried out again. He returned with several blankets which he silently dropped on to the sofa. Next time, he brought a tray of food and drink. Then he locked the door and slipped the key into his jacket pocket. 'We're going to be in here a long time,' he announced, lying down on the sofa. 'I think Julia should learn about love, starting right now.'

She pressed closer against my side, but Oswald looked at me in that special way, and when he pronounced my name I moved towards him as if mesmerised.

'Sit down, Julia, there, near the fire. I want you to be comfortable.' His voice was formal, as though she were a visitor to be entertained with the display of a cabinet of treasures. But then he smirked and added in a harsher tone: 'And I want you to have a good view. Come here, Mary.'

As soon as I was near enough, he pulled me down. For what felt like endless time, I was his partner in a demonstration of almost every possible method two people can use in the act of copulation. Julia sat without moving, totally absorbed. As far as I could tell, her eyes never left us. She did not even seem to blink. At last Oswald stood up. The fire was low and the room was cold.

'That's part of what love is.' He spoke only to Julia, turning his back on me and pulling on his shirt. 'I'm going to make the fire again, and eat something. Come and have some food.'

He was looking at her in that special way, and I was sure he was working the same magic on her that had enthralled me. It felt as if I did not exist for either of them. I sat up wearily and began to dress, not allowing myself to consider what my little sister was thinking. When I approached the table they turned from their mutual regard as though surprised that anyone else was in the room.

'Have some coffee,' Oswald said to her. 'I kept it hot in this jug.' He poured three cups, and for this recognition of my existence I felt pathetically grateful. 'We should rest now, that's why I brought the blankets.' He wrapped one of them around her shoulders, took one for himself, and threw one in my direction. 'There's a lot to learn about love,' Oswald said in a drowsy voice, lying down near the hearth, where the new logs were beginning to catch. 'Now go to sleep, both of you.' He pulled the blanket over his head and turned away. In a few minutes he was snoring. I looked towards Julia, but her eyes were closed and, in the way that sleep comes quickest at one's worst moments, I felt myself drift off almost as soon as I lay down on the rug.

I woke cramped and cold, disturbed by the sound of one of the cats scratching on the door outside. It was raining again, and early morning light slanting under the curtains emphasised every irregularity of the floorboards, and dust under the furniture. Carefully, I laid more wood on the ashy embers. Oswald was still swathed in his blanket. I wondered how he was able to breathe. Julia must have been restless in the night, because the upper half of her body was uncovered. I pulled the blanket gently over her shoulders then tiptoed across the room to the table. There was a jug of water there, and I poured some into the palm of my hand to wash my face. The only door leading out of the room was locked. Necessity forced me to take a large empty vase into the alcove by the bookcase to relieve myself. I did not want to think about what might happen next. I hoped Oswald would awaken bored with his freak, and open the door so that life could continue as if nothing had happened. Our previous constrained existence now seemed the epitome of freedom.

Perhaps it was the cat that woke him, or perhaps it was me. The next time I turned in his direction, I met a baleful glare and felt my heart constrict.

'How long have you been up?'

'Not long, only a few minutes,' I gabbled nervously. Why had I not appreciated that short period of solitude instead of foolishly hoping for his return to consciousness when, as I well knew by all the signs, today he was going to be in an evil and querulous temper? Though appalled by such involuntary submissiveness, I felt my whole body contract into a humble, placatory pose. Yet I ventured to ask: 'We won't keep Julia in here any longer, will we? It's been an adventure for her, sleeping with us on the floor, but I'm sure – ' I had not finished my sentence when Julia sat up. She turned abruptly from me as though flinching from a blow. This rejection hurt more than all the indignities of the night before.

Once upon a time, Julia and Mary and Oswald lived in a house in the middle of a wood. Julia and Mary were sisters, two princesses. The king and queen were dead and Oswald was the stable boy. (Or did I mean ostler, or groom? I chose groom because it made me think of bridegroom, and Oswald was the only young man I ever saw.)

I knew what cats and dogs got up to. I had watched the bull approach a cow, and horses in the fields bordering ours. But it took a little while to relate their simple, comparatively decent actions with what Oswald was doing to Mary. (The body Oswald manipulated, like a doll in the hands of an idiot, belonged to my sister.) They reminded me more of insects or acrobats or pictures of Oriental warriors and exotic dancers in our old encyclopaedias. It was frightening, exciting, and horribly fascinating to watch what a man and woman did.

The wind had died down and the rain had stopped. Darkness and silence isolated us from the rest of the world. Apart from the crackling fire and Oswald's curt commands, the only sounds were their grunts, gasps, sharp intakes of breath, occasional moans, and the noise flesh makes when it meets in blow or embrace.

Mary thought I never noticed her bruises and scratches, and was too young to sense the oppressive aura of sexuality that filled the house like escaping gas. Since our parents died she had treated me like an infant, and it had been easier to play the part assigned than to divert her attention from Oswald and let her see me as I was. In contrast to that obsessive preoccupation, she needed to believe I was an innocent. But the combination of my readings from the extensive library collected in the house, and the opportunity to observe and ponder her and Oswald's behaviour, had matured me beyond my years. It was only in physical development, and physical experience, that I remained childish. Oswald was quite different when we were alone than when Mary was with us. He often joked and did foolish things – in fact, I regarded him as a bit of a clown. I knew he was coarser and less intelligent than me, than either of us, but his company could be a relief after too much of Mary's reminiscing about our parents (whom I had almost forgotten), and her deep sighs as she gazed into my eyes.

The wicked ostler locked the sisters up and said he would do horrible things to them unless they promised . . . That's not right, because he is already doing things to Mary that might be horrible – but might be wonderful, and I want to know which. I want him to do the same to me and I think he guesses it. I'm sure Mary suspects, as well – that's why I won't look at her this morning. She has to believe he would abuse me; otherwise she would be forced to acknowledge that it is she who dominates, and makes him do whatever he does. But with me he will be completely different, I have no doubt of that.

Mary's nice, but a bit creepy. I think she really loves me. She knows I like to fool around, and sometimes get carried away and go too far, but she understands. She doesn't make a fuss. In fact, I think she likes the rough stuff. She'll make funny little movements, throw back her head and pretend to scream or laugh like a crazy, and if I still don't catch on, give me a pinch or a prod. Sometimes I think Julia knows about us – but how could she? She's only a kid. I could swear she was giving me the eye just then. She's a cute one – I wouldn't mind teaching her a thing or two.

I watched Julia put down her cup, move to where Oswald sat on one of the wooden chairs near the table, and pulling up her full red skirt and climbing on to his lap, decisively straddle him. Face pressed against his, she hugged him close. Her black-stockinged legs did not reach the floor. He stared mutely over her shoulder, as astonished as I was. His arms still hung limply by his sides.

'Things are going to be different this morning,' she announced a few minutes later in a cold, firm voice I had never heard before, fixing her gaze directly on him as she adjusted his clothes and pulled his arms up to clasp her round the waist. 'Leave Mary alone, Oswald. You'll do what I tell you now, not what she says.' I had the impression that her resolution wavered for a moment as her face flushed and she shifted slightly against him. Then she continued, 'First of all, get some more wood and build up the fire so that Mary won't be cold in here.

After that, go to the kitchen and make some hot food.' Abruptly, she threw back her head, then stood up and came towards me. 'Go on,' she ordered, turning to make sure he was obeying, before her hand gently touched my shoulder.

'My dear sister.' It was almost impossible to believe she was so young. Her voice was as charged with sorrow and pity as that of an old woman who has experienced every vicissitude of human existence. 'Oswald won't hurt you any more. You are free of him now, I can protect you. There's no need to submit to him ever again.' She looked searchingly at me, but I could not force my eyes to meet hers. I did not know whether I wanted to fall at her feet in a paroxysm of gratitude, or rush from the room to find Oswald, so that the two of us could murder her.

Oswald's cowed appearance, when he came back with a tray of food in his hands, dismayed me. Hopeless tears streamed from my eyes, and when Julia began to console me, I recognised that she had mastered us both.

'Come upstairs, Oswald,' she said later, after we had eaten. I was going to be denied even the final pleasure of watching him do the same with someone else as he had done with me. All that was left for the rest of my life would be memories.

Poor Mary. I long to make her better. I've felt so sorry for her. As soon as I've finished with Oswald, I'm going to take her away from here. There must be someone in the village who remembers our parents and will help us. She's twice my age, but I know now that I shall have to look after her for ever as if she were the little sister.

SELFLESS

They were walking through a landscape of small terraced hills with bright streams in the valleys between, which made Xie think of a painted scroll from classical times. When she and Yang had been posted to a nearby town, during their first year together, it had amazed her to see that such beauty could exist in the real world. Now, on holiday there with him and Shu, a colleague from the ministry, she was uncertain whether the remembered pleasures of first love, the gratification produced by painterly associations, or resignation and regret at the falling away since then, was the stronger feeling. Like millions of others in their country, she and Yang had endured much. But in spite of forced separations and other pressures, they had remained together, and now at last it seemed that they were being allowed to enjoy some of the pleasures of existence – such as this present holiday.

Shu was a thin, rather stiff-jointed woman a few years older than either of them, childless like herself and, as far as Xie knew, a widow. But until people had been acquainted for much longer, personal details were not discussed. Shu had been transferred to their province from the capital some months before, and no one knew whether it was a demotion or a promotion for her. Perhaps her husband had died in one of the purges. Perhaps he was still alive in some distant border area, banished to a work camp. Or perhaps they had divorced years ago.

As if he had learned nothing at all from the past and was still the excitable, ruddy-cheeked young man she had met at university, Yang would not stop talking about the time he and Xie used to walk through these same valleys. He poured out one story after another until Xie felt a combination of irritation, embarrassment and unease. She was not sure she liked the idea of Shu learning so many facts about them. Who knew how she might use such information in the future?

Bowing her head slightly to one side and darting secret glances from the corner of her eye, Xie tried not to let Shu realise that she was being observed. To her surprise, instead of catching a gleeful or malicious expression on the older woman's face, Shu looked absolutely desolate, as if about to burst into tears, and stumbled on the stony path, grazing her leg. To Xie, it seemed as if she had willed the fall, the way a child will make itself trip over to attract attention or interrupt a parent's or teacher's reprimands. And like a child, she burst into noisy tears and lamentations.

'How awful!' she moaned. 'Look, I've cut myself. The soil here is so polluted. I'm sure to get gangrene and die.'

'Of course you won't,' Xie said, surprised, and Yang and she tried to convince Shu that it was only a superficial graze. She started to get some water from the stream to wash the dirt away, but Shu shouted out that surely they must want her to die if they thought she would put such contaminated liquid, which everyone knew was as full of germs as a sewer, on to an open wound.

This sort of behaviour was extraordinary. Only young children indulged in such undisguised self-pity. Until now, Xie had regarded Shu as a strong and admirable member of their team at work.

'Let me tell you about something really strange that happened when Xie and I lived here,' Yang began enthusiastically, in an effort to change the subject.

'I know I'll get gangrene and die!' Shu ignored him and moaned even louder, then lay down by the side of the path, insisting she felt too ill to walk a step further.

'Try to stand up,' Yang pleaded. 'We can't stay here. The village is only round the next bend.'

164

'It's too far, I'll never make it. If I walk, the dust will settle on my leg and the gangrene will start. I'll be dead in a couple of days.'

'Let me cover it with my scarf,' Xie offered. But this was received no better than her earlier suggestion. Husband and wife stared at each other, nonplussed, then Xie put an arm around Shu's shoulder, smiled broadly and said, 'You are a tease! Come on, I know you're only pretending.'

'I'm not pretending,' Shu howled. 'I'm going to die, I know I am.'

'Well,' Yang said decisively. 'There's only one thing left. Do you remember that course we did in emergency first-aid?'

'No . . . ' Shu answered in a quavering voice, looking up at him from where she huddled on the ground, tears glistening along her eyelashes.

'I don't either,' added Xie.

'Don't you remember how it said that when there's no other way to disinfect a wound, urine is better than nothing at all?'

'Urine?' Shu's voice became lower and softer. It almost sounded as if a giggle were lurking behind the tears.

'Yes. Urine. I can even recite the paragraph by heart.' His expression altered until he looked exactly like the exemplary citizen on a propaganda poster or illustrating one of the many manuals they had to study, and the voice that emerged from his stiffened lips sounded distorted, as if through a loudspeaker. '"In case of emergency, a male comrade should urinate on an open wound if no other disinfecting agent is available."'

'Only a male comrade,' Shu tittered.

'I never thought I'd see it happen,' Xie remarked. Maybe in a war – but certainly not on holiday.'

'Let's go there, behind those bushes.' Shu had scrambled to her feet. 'We should do it as soon as possible.'

'You stay here, Xie,' Yang commanded. 'No need for you to come with us.'

'I'll be glad to have a rest,' she said, stooping to pick a stem of flowering grass that caught her eye.

Xie was intrigued to note how dramatically Shu's mood had improved, when she and Yang returned. 'That's done me a lot of good, I'm sure,' Shu confided. 'If you give me your scarf, I'll wrap it around my leg and we can carry on with our walk.' It was still early in the afternoon, and Xie was glad their excursion would not be shortened. Shu seemed even more eager to keep going than before her accident.

Yang was carrying their food in his haversack, and they stopped to eat near a grove of trees at the top of a hill. Afterwards, Shu complained that her leg was hurting again. 'Maybe I need another treatment.'

'Yes, maybe you do,' he concurred.

Xie doubted the necessity, so soon after the first, but was impressed by Yang's willingness to be of service. She watched Shu hobble away, leaning on her husband's arm.

'That should do it,' Yang said, adjusting his waistband as they returned.

'You can't be too careful,' Shu answered demurely. Xie was beginning to wonder if she really liked Shu, and whether this holiday together had been a good idea.

'How is your leg today?' she asked next morning.

'Yang has been an angel,' Shu replied. 'A few more treatments and I'm sure it won't turn into gangrene.'

'Today's the last day of the holiday, so you'll be able to go to the infirmary when we get back.'

'Yes, it is the last day,' Shu repeated in a dreamy, half-regretful tone. 'I haven't enjoyed myself so much for ages.'

There was a slyness about her which Xie had never noticed before – though it was hard to know exactly what had changed her opinion. Today, it was Xie who wanted to talk about their early days, as they set out for a final walk, but Yang seemed preoccupied, and she soon fell silent. 'We could go up there,' Shu insisted. 'Come on, Yang. I'm sure another treatment would do me good.'

*

Shu worked in a different section of the ministry, so it was usually only at departmental meetings that the two women met. Xie was surprised, after that week's meeting, by Shu's insistent invitation to a teahouse for a drink and a talk. Yang had been sent on a tour of inspection across the province as soon as they got back from holiday, so there was no need to hurry home to cook a meal.

'How is everything, Shu?' she said, when they had been served. It was very noisy, and she had to raise her voice to ask. 'Has your leg healed yet?'

'Yang sent me this letter,' Shu said abruptly. 'Read it.' She thrust a sheet of paper into Xie's hand.

'Why should he write to you?' Xie murmured, quite sure that she did not want to read what he had written. She handed the paper back to Shu. 'It's your letter. If Yang had wanted me to see it, he would have shown it to me.'

Shu gulped down her tea, then stood up and pushed her way through the tables without saying anything further. Xie was left to pay for them both.

Yang returned some weeks later with a bottle of fine rice wine a satisfied local manager had presented to him. Xie cooked a special meal and made their room warmer than usual.

'How have things been at work?' he asked.

'Oh, perfectly all right.'

'And Shu – how is she?'

'Her leg is quite healed,' Xie replied, head turned to one side and gaze downcast, but glancing at him from the corner of her eye.

'It was foolish of me to talk in front of her about how happy we had been, there in the hills. It made her feel very sad and sorry for herself.'

'Yes,' said Xie. 'I noticed.'

'I had to do something to cheer her up,' Yang said after another silence, another sip of rice wine.

'Yes,' said Xie. 'I noticed.'

'But I wrote her a letter to say how glad I was her leg had healed, and that she wouldn't need me to give her any more treatments.'

'Yes,' said Xie. 'How selfless you were.'

Dr Clock's Last Case

'Dr Clock Cures All Ills', read the card he gave her as soon as she crossed the threshold, and she put it in the side pocket of her handbag and believed what it said.

'Come to bed with me, and I'll make you better.' He began to undo the buttons of his greasy tweed jacket and trousers, grunting slightly as he strained over his paunch to reach them, long-haired grey head turned away as if never doubting for one moment that she would do whatever he ordered.

It wasn't really a bed, but a couch, upholstered in the same faded blue woven stuff that covered its pillows, standing against one wall of what he referred to as his consulting chamber. A tall narrow window, blurred by years of dirt, opened on to an inner courtyard, and that afternoon the room was even darker than usual as rain fell from an overcast, grey sky.

Lucy still wore her coat – a military-style black mackintosh. A slight fair woman of about thirty, she hesitated in the centre of the room, watching him undress. She felt satisfied but tired, as if after arriving at a destination sought for years. Everything she wore today was black or some other muted, sombre shade, except for her underpants, which were a vivid neon purple.

'Come on now, put that handbag down. Get your clothes off. You look like a prison visitor.' Dr Clock, shapely fat knees revealed between high socks and long green-and-white striped boxer shorts, tutted impatiently. 'You want me to cure you, don't you? Well, let's get on with it.'

'Can you really cure all ills?' she asked wonderingly, twisting round to unzip her skirt. Everything seemed so matter-of-fact that obviously he could. Otherwise, why would she be here?

'Headache, heartache, hernia, haemorrhoids, hopelessness, or any other letter you like. Just get undressed and believe what I tell you.' Dr Clock was naked now, but seemed no different than when he had opened the door fully clothed. His compact body looked as warm and healthy and unselfconscious as a rubber doll's. 'You'll be cold, I suppose,' he muttered, lighting the gas fire. 'I like that purple.' He picked up her nylon pants and draped them over the desk light. The room became a grotto. 'Now come here, next to me.' He sat on the couch and patted the grubby surface. 'Tell me what's the matter.'

There had been no chance to examine his face. An impression of paleness, of profuse greyish hair and rather bulging pale eyes was all she had taken in, and though sitting next to him now, she felt no urge to scrutinise him more closely.

'Come on, tell me what's the matter,' he repeated. 'That's why you rang my bell and came here, isn't it? That's why you took my card and read it and put it somewhere safe. Lie back, and tell me everything.'

She stretched out on the rough fabric and he bent over and peered at the middle of her body, as if the truth would issue from there. 'I saw your advertisement on a noticeboard, and came here straight away, hoping you'd see me,' she began. 'Yes, yes,' he said encouragingly, placing one hand gently on her belly. 'And why did you think I could help you?' His head was bent so low he seemed to be more interested in how she smelt than what she said, yet Lucy was sure he was listening intently. 'I need someone to help me. Something is wrong with me, I know.'

The heat from the gas fire and its flickering light on the purpled ceiling made her drowsy. It seemed years since she'd been so comfortable. 'Open your legs,' Dr Clock said. 'I want you to talk to me, because I know that's what you want to do. You don't want to listen. I don't have to say anything. You know what's the matter.' Compliance was confirmation of his

170

diagnosis. Of course she knew what was the matter with her and what she wanted. Hip-joints rolled flexed legs easily outwards as he bent even lower and fastened his mouth around the parted lips of her vagina and began a soft regular sucking like a baby at the nipple.

'I thought something was wrong with me when I was out there,' Lucy mused, watching the patterns on the walls and ceiling, distanced like all the complexities of her life outside this room. 'But in here there doesn't seem to be much wrong, after all.' She ended on an interrogatory note, but Dr Clock did not lift his head to reply, and after a short pause she continued. That gentle, rhythmic pumping was like a completion, as though if it could continue even after she left this room, if somehow it were possible to take his lips away and leave the rest of him behind, she would be invulnerable to every pain and uncertainty for the rest of her life. 'I'm not sick, am I?' The question did not need an answer. The knots in her joints and intestines were loosening like flaccid snakes after coupling. Dr Clock's mouth increased its grip, a hand moved under her hips and tilted her pelvis slightly.

'If I could feel like this all the time, nothing would hurt me, isn't that so?' Lucy asked. 'All the problems would go away.' She vaguely sensed a contradiction, but was beginning not to care whether she remained consistent with earlier statements, or even went on talking. But Dr Clock obviously would not tolerate silence. He lifted his head and ordered, 'Go on, you haven't said anything yet.'

'Leave me alone,' she gasped. 'Stop telling me what to do. Everyone tells me what to do, I can't stand it!' She half pulled herself up, but firmly, gently, he pressed her back down. 'Everyone bullies me,' she sobbed, in the grip of a tantrum such as dimly remembered from early childhood. She tried to fight him off, screaming, 'I hate you, you've always stopped me from doing what I want, you never let me have anything. I hate you. You're like everyone else, they're all against me.'

The purple light seemed glacial. 'I'm all alone and so

171

unhappy!' Tears of self-pity softened her anger. If only he would comfort her she would forgive anything. 'Nobody has ever loved me – never – nobody – and now you're the same. I thought you'd cure me, but you're only making me even sicker.' It was true – nodes of pain flared from every part of her body. She was frightened by their clanging, grinding intensity, and the conviction that she was about to die. 'Forgive me,' she pleaded, arms outstretched. 'I'll do whatever you say if only you'll forgive me and be kind to me. I can't bear it otherwise.'

'Get up now,' Dr Clock said. 'I want you to beat me. Here. He pulled the leather belt from his trousers. 'Hit me. Take it out on me. You don't want me to forgive you – it's just that you're too frightened to punish me. Well, go ahead – hit me.'

'No, no,' she begged. 'I do want you to forgive me, truly, please. No one has ever forgiven me. I'm a great sinner.'

'All right, then. If you really want to be punished, I'll do it for you.'

The first lash shocked, but the next blows infuriated her. 'Give that to me,' she shouted, trying to dodge the strap and get it away from him. 'I do hate you, it's true. I do want to beat you. I want to kill you. I want to kill everyone, because nobody ever forgives me or loves me. Give me that strap, you bastard.' Blinded by fury, she still could not see what he looked like, but it did not matter; he had become father, grandfathers, uncles, grown-up smirking cousins, every man who'd ever teased and played with and rejected her.

'Hit me,' he said, surrendering the strap and waiting passively, half turned away. She lashed at his back and shoulders, but in that position he seemed androgynous, epicene, more like a plump middle-aged woman than a man. She stopped and frowned and blinked, shaking sweat-heavy hair from her eyes. Surely it was her mother standing there? In just that pose her mother had stood and stared into the gas fire at home when Lucy was a child, halted in her dressing by some reverie. Would it be possible to hit her mother? Did she want to?

'Are you my mother?' she asked in a low, nervous voice.

'Mother?' Whoever it was, the figure did not turn. 'For God's sake, tell me if you're my mother,' Lucy pleaded. 'Why don't you turn round? Don't you love me? Mother – ' She fell on to her knees and began to beat her head on the floor. 'Mother, Mother, Mother,' she moaned. 'Do I want to hit my mother?' It was too terrible a dilemma to bear.

'You don't have to hit me if you don't want to,' Dr Clock said, and put a warm arm round her trembling shoulders.

'I can't kill my mother,' Lucy cried. 'It would be suicide.' He helped her on to the couch again and stroked her, and she immediately fell into an exhausted sleep.

A few minutes later she woke, alert and refreshed. He sat cross-legged in the armchair opposite, wearing a multicoloured silk kimono. 'Read this,' he said. It was another card, in the same style as the first, but with a different message: 'Dr Clock Never Stops'.

'Recite the alphabet for me,' he commanded, as she studied the cryptic inscription.

'The alphabet?' she repeated, confused.

'Come on, start saying it.' He didn't look at her, but pensively twirled a loose thread in the hem of the kimono.

'A–B–C –' Lucy began, barely able to believe that she was complying with his demands. 'D–E–F–G –' It was impossible to think about anything else while reciting these letters, saying these words which took over the entire mind like a meditation exercise. 'Aych, Eye, Jay, Kay – ' She was aware of nothing except these letters, and his controlling power. 'M–N–O–P–Q–R–S – ' Eyes fixed on the purple-tinged figure in the armchair, she crouched down and slowly began to crawl forward. 'T–U–V–W–X–Y–Z.' When she had reached the last letter her face was level with his knees. She sat on the floor at his feet and laid her head on his lap.

'Kiss my cock,' he said, shifting to open the kimono. Lucy closed her eyes and parted her lips and felt a thick, half erect penis slide between them. It stiffened and enlarged in her mouth; she gagged as it pressed deeper into her throat. 'Kneel,' he said, pulling away, when she was about to suffocate. He knelt behind her, a breast clasped in each hand.

'Ah!' she groaned at his penetration.

'Now say the alphabet,' he ordered. 'But do it backwards.'

'I can't,' she moaned. 'Leave me alone.'

'Come on, begin.' He emphasised his words with a deep thrust.

'Z–Y–X–W– ' With each letter she became more burning and open, fluttered and dragged him further inside her. By contrast, he barely moved, only to use his penis as a sort of prod when she stopped for too long, or began to droop towards the floor. There was no way to measure the duration of this alphabet. Between some letters aeons passed, as if she had sunk into the heart of a mountain of black basalt which would have to be eroded away by time and climate before she would be released to intone the next sound. She had never felt so content.

'Now stand up,' he said when she reached 'A', abruptly drawing back, wrapping the kimono close and sitting down again. Dazed, Lucy looked around the room. She could barely remember who or where she was, or why she knelt there, arms stiff and trembling, knees chafed by the rough carpeting. 'Tell me why you came to see me. What do you think I can do for you?'

She tried to break through this present moment and remember. 'Cure me, that's it,' she said at last. 'I want you to cure me. I want you to stop me from suffering. I want to escape from all the passions that torment me. I want my life.'

'Life?' he repeated.

'Maybe that's not exactly what I mean,' she amended uncertainly. Things seemed to be getting worse. 'I want to stop being affected by everything that happened in the past. And sometimes I think that future events are sending their influences back at me. How can I be kinder to anyone else than I am

174

to myself?' She snorted with inappropriate, ironic laughter. 'Maybe I don't have the temperament for my beliefs.'

'I am not Doctor Spock.'

'Who's Dr Spock?' she wondered. 'You're Dr Clock, aren't you?'

'Dr Clock, the lollipop,' he answered gleefully, and leaned forward to put one hand on each side of her head and clamp her startled face into his groin again. Roughly pushing his rigid penis into her mouth, he discharged a thick, hot, copious stream of semen. 'Swallow it,' he commanded sternly. 'It's your first dose of my medicine.'

Her throat convulsed, then as the viscous liquid mixed with her own saliva she tried to savour its faint saltiness. 'This is your medicine, is it?' she mumbled abstractedly when she could speak. 'I don't see how it's going to cure me.'

'It's life, my dear lady. You say you want life – that's the essence of life, or so I understand. What better medicine could I give you?'

'I don't see that things are any different in here than anywhere else,' Lucy said, petulant and bitter. She stood up and leaned against the mantelpiece to stare into the gas fire's incandescence. It wasn't the taste in her mouth making her feel sick, but intense disappointment. 'What's the difference between you and all the others? You've only made me feel worse. I thought there was some hope somewhere – ' She turned away, but the tears would not hold back, and the gas fire flashed and sparkled through her lashes. She rushed towards the couch and pulled the heavy, square cushions on top of herself, howling with grief.

Such an outburst could not sustain itself against his uninvolvement. 'So I disappointed you, did I, Lucy? But you didn't come to me for gratification, did you, but to be cured.'

It was difficult to say what she had expected. 'I thought it would be wonderful,' she murmured after a pause, ashamed by such an admission.

'You know better than that, or you wouldn't have come here,'

175

he asserted. 'You didn't come just to be fucked. You said you wanted to escape from your passions.'

'I suppose so,' she concurred bleakly. She had not imagined that escape from passions would involve their re-enactment.

'Dr Clock unpicks the lock,' he stated in a confident tone of voice. 'Look up at the ceiling.' He stood behind his desk now, adjusting a small projector. By switching off the lamp, eliminating the purple glow of her underwear and leaving the orange light from the gas fire as the only illumination, he completely altered the atmosphere of the room.

'What are those things?' she asked, unable to decipher the mass of squirming, pullulating objects pushing blindly against each other.

'They could be cells, or bacteria, or they could be maggots in the earth or in a wound – or they could be larger animals, even people, I'm not sure. It's films of all those things, superimposed on each other. It doesn't seem to make any difference what the scale of life is or even what the motive is supposed to be. It looks the same from far enough away.'

'But what does that mean, what are you trying to say?'

'You decide what you want it to mean, and it will mean just that. You can't help but be right.'

The image covered the ceiling. Lucy looked upwards, held by the inexplicable activity. The colours flushed from cool to bloody, then back again, like a mass migration, the speeded-up view of a battlefield from high in space, or the changing pattern of seasons on another planet. It repelled and calmed her at the same time.

'I think this is cancer cells reproducing,' he remarked in an explanatory, schoolmasterly sort of voice.

'I suppose it could be.' She was beginning to feel bored and tired. 'I think I'll get dressed.'

'Yes, we've had enough for today,' he agreed, as she found her clothes and put them on by the light of the still-continuing film, which now might have been spores exploding open, or a distant view of land under heavy bombardment.

Searching through her handbag for lipstick and comb, Lucy saw the knife. She had bought it last summer on holiday, fascinated by the ornate handle and long blade, and it had lain forgotten in one of the bag's many compartments ever since. Without the transfiguring purple glow, the room had become as shabby as before. Dr Clock switched off the projector and moved round the desk until he stood in front of her.

For the first time she was looking directly at his face, which gave her the unnerving sensation of being transported into the future, studying the reflection of her own features as they would be in about twenty years. They both had the same anxious, staring blue eyes with puffy sockets, the same short nose and receding chin. Her hair would be as grey as his then, and float about her head in the same way. The differences were superficial: the effects of gender, weight and time which had dragged down his jowls and the corners of mouth and eyes. She was not merely frightened, but also deeply disillusioned by their resemblance. If she had looked at him properly, nothing would have happened, she was quite sure.

'When will you come again, dear lady?' the ridiculous old creature enquired in an unctuous voice. 'I'm sure we can make a lot of progress, in time. Don't forget, Dr Clock cures all ills!' he tittered, and stared calculatingly, boldly, into her eyes.

Lucy was closing the last button of her mackintosh. Pale hair tied severely back, insignificant body encased in the stiff garment, heavy black bag over one arm, she did look rather like a prison visitor, as he had commented when she arrived.

'Dr Clock gets a shock,' she hissed, furious with him but even more with herself, as she swooped her hand into the bag, brought out the knife, and pushed it into his chest where the kimono had fallen open. It sank between two ribs, up to the hilt. She had struck as accurately as a trained assassin.

His eyes opened even further. 'It is a shock,' he gasped, slumping slowly down and forward until he lay at her feet. She bent to pull the knife brutally out of his body, then wiped the blade clean on his kimonoed haunch and dropped it back into her bag. He had fallen between her and the door.

'Dr Clock, the stumbling block,' she said gleefully, stepping over him. There was no sign that she had ever been in the room, no one passed her in the long dark hall, and she met no one as she let herself out of the building and walked quickly away.